'What in the hell happened to you, old man?' asked Brogan McNally as he gazed down at the battered body of an elderly, bearded man sitting dejectedly on a tree stump. 'Looks to me like you had some kinda accident or somethin'.'

'I reckon you could say that,' came the grimaced reply. 'First time I've ever been beaten though.'

'First time?' queried Brogan, dismounting from his horse to help the old man to his feet.

'Yeh! Normally they just take my money an' leave me alone.' The old man gingerly felt his bruised face and winced as he looked around. 'Looks like they stole my mule too – bastards!'

'Sounds to me like you've been through this kinda thing before,' said Brogan.

'A few times,' admitted the old man. 'But they never beat me before.'

'I don't pretend to know what it's all about,' said Brogan, shaking his head. 'Can't say as I care that much either. Where you headed?'

'Aint much point in goin' nowheres now, I guess I'll just have to head back for town.' He looked

5

around again and sighed heavily. 'What the hell they want to steal my mule for? Come to think on it, they weren't the usual outfit, I didn't recognize any of 'em.'

'Regular outfit! You mean you know 'em?'

'Not this lot,' muttered the old man. 'T'others wouldn't've beat me or taken my mule. They know darned well I would've given 'em the money. I ain't no hero, 'specially since it ain't my money.'

'Look, old timer!' Brogan sighed. 'I ain't no mind reader an' like I said, I ain't really that interested, it's your problem, not mine, but you sure don't look in any condition to walk anywhere. You can ride with me if you want to. That is if I'm going in the same direction.'

'So where you goin'?'

'South. Don't know where to an' I care even less.'

The old man looked Brogan up and down smiled and slightly. 'You look like a saddlebum an' you smell like a saddlebum, but you sure don't act like a saddlebum. I ain't never met one yet what'd lift a finger to help anyone. No sir, saddlebums is more likely to rob a body than help him. Won't do you no good though, somebody already beat you to it.'

'I ain't lookin' to rob nobody,' said Brogan. 'Yeh, I guess I am a saddlebum an' I'm kinda proud of it. I ain't never robbed nobody in my life – an' you can believe that or not an' I don't care which. Now, quit jawin' about me an' decide if'n you wanna ride with me, smell an' all.'

'I guess I don't smell too sweet either!' The old man grinned. 'OK, Mister I got me this feeling I can trust you. Don't know why, but you don't seem like the usual saddlebum. South is the direction I wannna go. My name's Cummins, Pete Cummins. What's yours, or don't you want anyone to know?'

'It ain't no secret,' said Brogan. 'McNally, Brogan McNally. Just call me Brogan, I don't go for the "Mister" bit.'

'Brogan! OK, Brogan, let's go.'

Brogan mounted his horse and held out his arm to help Pete up behind him. 'I know I said I did't care what all this was about,' he said. 'I am kinda curious though – I guess you could call it plain nosey – 'specially since you seem to accept it as somethin' that happens regularly.'

'Too darned regular, just lately,' agreed Pete, settling himself. 'Ain't my money they took though, that would be plain loco if'n I was to let 'em take my money. Not that I got that much for anyone to take. Naw, they took the wages for the miners up in the hills.'

Brogan grunted. 'An' what's an old man like you doin' with miners' wages?'

'Takin' it out to 'em of course ! Why else?'

Brogan shrugged. 'Sounds kinda crazy to me.'

'I gotta agree with you on that!' replied Pete. 'An' I guess I must be crazy to be doin' the job, but it pays well an' nobody else'll give me much work.'

'By the sounds of things, I'd say it pays better for them what took it off you. How much was it?'

' 'Bout two thousand dollars.'

'That much!' Brogan whistled. 'Nice pickin's any day.'

'Yeh, nice pickin's,' agreed Pete. 'This is the fourth time in three months. Mister Mitchell ain't gonna be to pleased.'

'Mitchell?'

'Seth Mitchell. He owns the mine.'

'So why don't he take out the wages?'

'Too busy, I guess. Big man in these parts, oughta be, he owns most of it.'

'So why does he let an old man like you risk his life takin' wages out to his mines?'

Pete laughed, drily. 'That's easy! I'm the cheapest an' besides why should he risk gettin' killed? Ain't nobody gonna worry over much 'bout me. Most times I get through, but these past few months ain't been so easy.'

Brogan nudged his horse forward, content to let her go at her usual plodding pace, since he was in no particular hurry. 'Strikes me this Mitchell'd save more money if'n he'd use more men, men able to look after 'emselves,' he observed. 'Not that I'm sayin' you can't look after yoursel', you understand.'

'I can hold my own, probably better'n most in this kinda country,' said Pete. 'But I ain't no gunman.'

'So why don't he use better armed men?'

'He tried that!' Pete laughed. 'Twice! Both times both men an' money disappeared without trace. So he figured that if he was gonna lose his money anyhow, he might as well use me. He knows I ain't about to hightail it, no matter how much I'm carryin'. 'Sides, I know this territory better than any man alive. If I get wind of trouble up ahead, I can usually hide up or find another way round. It ain't easy, but there's ways.'

'Well I guess that you an' this Mitchell know your own buisness,' said Brogan. 'You say the town's up ahead. What's it called?'

'Abbotsville,' said Pete. 'It's a fair sized town, most of it owned by Mitchell. Named after his uncle, Mitchell inherited it 'bout ten years ago. I gotta admit he's done a lot for this territory. Old man Abbot didn't seem to care that much, but Mitchell has really built the place up.'

'Don't mean no disrespect to him,' said Brogan, 'but I don't trust any man that's too powerful.'

'There's a good many as'd agree with you,' said Pete. 'But he's a business man, don't let sentiment stand in his way. Maybe he's too hard an' businesslike sometimes, but most folk get by.'

'Maybe!' muttered Brogan. 'How far?'

'Eight miles, maybe nine,' replied Pete.

They rode slowly for about twenty minutes when Brogan suddenly stopped and listened intently. 'We got company not far ahead,' he whispered. 'Get off an' hide somewheres.'

'How the hell you know that?' asked Pete. 'I don't see nothin' an' I sure don't hear nothin'.'

'Just take my word for it,' said Brogan. 'I could be wrong, but it ain't often I am. Now, you hide up while I go take a look.'

Pete slid off the horse and looked around,

rather bewildered.

'Don't see how you can tell,' he whispered. 'A whole army could hide up in those trees an' not be heard or seen.'

'Pete!' Brogan grinned, also getting off the horse. 'I been a drifter all my life – I lost count of just how long that is – an' I got a sorta sixth sense 'bout these things. 'Sides, signs are clear enough, to me at any rate.'

'Then I guess I'll just have to take your word for it,' said Pete. 'Maybe I can help.'

'Best way you can help is to do like I said an' hide up!' said Brogan. 'I prefer workin' on my own.'

'You're the boss!' Pete grinned.

'That's right!' agreed Brogan. 'Take my horse with you, an' keep quiet till I get back.'

Pete led the horse into a thick clump of bushes and Brogan, rifle in hand, crept forward. After he had gone about fifty yards he crouched behind a bush and peered through it. Below him, just off the trail, were four men, three of them lounging about whilst the fourth appeared to be counting money.

'Two thousand one hundred!' the man counting exclaimed. 'Told you he'd have about that much.'

'So what do we do now?' asked one of the others.

'We can't go back to workin' for Mitchell, that's for sure,' came the reply. 'That old man'll recognize us, nothin' more certain.'

'I said we shoulda killed him!' said another.

'Maybe we should,' agreed the man with the

money. 'Yeh, I reckon we should've. If he ain't alive, there ain't nobody can put the finger on us.'

'All we gotta do is wait here, he's gotta come this way back to town. He won't be no trouble.'

Brogan had heard enough. 'You ain't waitin' for nobody!' he barked, emerging from behind the bush, rifle at the ready. Sudenly his rifle fired its deadly message as one of them tried to grab his gun. The man gurgled slightly and sank to the ground as the others stared helplessly. 'One down, three to go!' grated Brogan. 'Who's next?' The men did not move. 'Nobody? Very wise.' He moved slowly forward. 'Keep your hands where I can see 'em,' he warned. 'You musta thought this was your lucky day. Two thousand ain't bad. Sorry to have spoiled it for you. Normally I wouldn't bother, but I found this old man up on the trail, badly beaten. I don't like folk what pick on old men. Now you with the money, place it on that rock and back off. Oh, an' leave your guns there too. I ain't sayin' as I don't trust you, I don't. Back off over there, away from those horses.'

'This ain't none of your business!' said the man laying the money and his gun on the rock.

'True,' agreed Brogan. 'Kinda looks like I just made it my business though don't it?'

'Saddlebum!' sneered one of the others. 'You probably killed the old man an' now you is gonna take the money.'

'If I did kill him, it sure saved you a job,' said Brogan, indicating that the other two lay down their guns, which they did. 'But he's right behind me!' He called back. 'OK, Pete, I know you is there. Thought I told you to stay where you was?'

'You must have eyes up your arse!' Pete laughed, emerging from his cover. 'I thought I could be quieter'n a mouse.'

'A mouse!' Brogan laughed. 'Pete, I reckon I could hear a fly land on a lump of shit from a hundred yards!'

'I'm beginnin' to believe it too!' Pete laughed.

'Go get your money,' said Brogan. 'An' bring them guns over here.' Pete did as instructed, not bothering to count the money, since he was not sure how much there should be, besides which when it came to counting, he had difficulty with anything greater than ten. 'Now find some cord or twine or somethin' an tie these three up, that one won't be no bother.' He nodded at the dead man.

'What you done with my Esmerelda?' demanded Pete, going to the horses and finding only a rope.

'Esmerelda?' queried one of the men.

'Yeh, Esmerelda, my mule!' repeated Pete.

'It's over there!' said one of the others. 'We turned it loose.'

Pete was about to go and look for his mule, when Brogan stopped him. 'You can find her later,' he snapped. 'First, get them tied up! Right now they is more important.'

'To you maybe!' responded Pete. 'OK, I'll tie 'em up.' He roughly pushed each man's arms behind their backs and lashed them firmly, using a large knife to cut the rope. Only when Brogan was satisfied that their bonds were secure did he nod to Pete.

'Esmerelda!' Pete called. 'Where are you, you stubborn critter?' He ran, remarkably fast, in the direction the man had indicated and, after a couple of minutes, returned with a seemingly reluctant Esmerelda. 'She's OK!' Pete grinned.

'Glad to hear it,' muttered Brogan. 'Now, we take them back to town with us.'

'Hang 'em from that tree is what I say!' grated Pete.

'That won't do no good,' said Brogan. 'You three, lie on the ground!' They did as they were told. 'Pete, help me get this one on one of the horses.' He pointed at the dead man.

Dead men are very much a dead weight, and they struggled for a while getting him into position, eventually securing his arms and legs to the girth strap. 'Thought I recognized him,' said Pete. 'I saw him the other day in Mitchell's office.' He looked hard at the others. 'Yeh, now I know who you are. If I remember right, you all came to work for Mitchell about a month ago.'

'So what?' snapped one.

'So nothin',' said Pete. 'Mister Mitchell may be a good business man, but he sure ain't no judge of men. I only got to look at you to know you couldn't be trusted.'

'Maybe you'll get a bonus!' sneered another.

'Maybe we should,' agreed Pete. 'It's Brogan here what earned it though.'

'Brogan!' snarled the man. 'I'll remember that name!'

'For all the good it'll do you,' said Brogan. 'Right, on your horses, Pete'll give you a hand.'

The men struggled to their feet and allowed Pete to help them on their horses and Brogan checked their bonds again and seemed satisfied. 'I reckon Mitchell'll be glad to see you,' said Pete.

'We shoulda killed you when we had the chance,' muttered one, looking at Pete.

'Yeh, maybe you should've,' agreed Pete, laughing. 'But you didn't an' now the laugh's on you.'

'Right, move out, nice an' slow,' ordered Brogan. 'Remember, you won't get very far tied up, an' I'm a darned good shot with this Winchester, so don't try nothin'.' The men simply scowled and nudged their horses forward. Pete clambered on to his protesting mule, cursing at her to stand still and followed them back on to the trail.

'I reckon Mitchell should give you a reward,' said Pete. 'He's a hard headed man though, I think you'll have to haggle with him.'

'I don't haggle with nobody,' said Brogan. 'What, if anythin', he chooses to give me I'll take an' be glad of it. I am kinda low on funds at the moment.'

'Take my advice,' said Pete. 'Haggle! Don't take the first offer he makes, if he makes one at all.'

'I'll think about it,' said Brogan. 'Could just as easy take that two thousand an' get the hell outa here right now.'

'But you won't!' Pete grinned. 'Like I said, I ain't a bad judge of men, an' you don't strike me as the kind who would do somethin' like that. Not that I'd blame you if you did, but Mitchell'll have a posse after you straight away.'

'An' like I said,' said Brogan, 'I ain't never took anythin' what don't belong to me an' I ain't never been wanted by no sheriff or nobody an' I'm too old to start now.'

'Then you is a fool!' hissed one of the men.

'It ain't me what's headin' for the jail right now!' Brogan laughed. 'It's you, so who's the fool?'

'Bastard!' hissed the man.

'Probably!' Brogan agreed. 'Don't rightly know if my ma an' pa was ever married or not an' can't say as I care much either.'

They rode slowly for about another three quarters of an hour and eventually they were overlooking the town of Abbotsville. As Pete had said, it was a fair sized town and, from where they were, they looked down on to a wide main street with four smaller streets off. At the far end were some paddocks, perhaps ten or twelve, in two of which were a few horses, but the others were empty. In the countryside around the town could be seen grazing cattle.

'I seen bigger towns,' said Brogan. 'But I also seen plenty a lot smaller.'

'Yeh, there's bigger,' admitted Pete, 'but not in these parts.'

'A town is a town,' mused Brogan. 'Places I try to avoid if I possibly can. I don't find 'em very healthy places.'

'What you mean by that?'

'What I say. It's mainly on account of me an' sheriffs not gettin' on too well. Almost all of 'em don't seem to like my company an' usually suggest that I move on.'

'An' do you?'

'Sometimes I do an' sometimes I don't. It all depends on how the mood takes me. I suppose that most times I do move on, there don't usually seem much point in arguin'. What's your sheriff like?'

'Oh, he ain't so bad.' Pete grinned broadly. 'For the most part he runs an orderly town, but he can't make any big decisions without Mitchell's say-so.'

'That figures!' Brogan laughed. 'Bought an' paid for.'

'Matt Dempster he's called,' said Pete. 'Big man, knows how to handle himself in a fight – not that many usually choose to fight him. Handy with a gun too, so they tell me, although I ain't never seen him use one.'

'I might as well pick me up a few supplies while I'm here,' said Brogan. 'Then I suppose I'll be on my way.'

'Not till you've seen Mitchell. He owes you, you make sure you get what you're due for.'

'We'll see!' Brogan grinned.

It took longer to reach Abbotsville than expected. The trail from where they had looked down on the town proved very narrow, steep and twisting and, to make sure that their prisoners did not take the opportunity to make a run for it,

Brogan told Pete to lead the way. Eventually they were on flat ground and within about half a mile of the town.

Their arrival created a fair amount of interest, not least from other men who, according to Pete, were all in the employ of Mitchell. The men largely ignored Brogan and Pete, calling out to the three men, who sat sullenly and did not reply. A couple of the braver ones looked at the body on the horse, lifted his head and whistled.

'Amos!' one said. 'What happened to him?'

'I shot him!' replied Brogan.

'What the hell for?'

'Didn't have much choice!'

'Sheriff's office is halfway up the street,' said Pete. 'I guess you'll all find out about it pretty soon.'

The crowd followed them to the sheriff's office, where he was ready for them, grunting as he examined the body and tested the ropes around the wrists of the others.

'Better get 'em inside!' he said. 'There'd better be a good reason for this, Pete.'

'There's a good reason,' assured Pete, helping each man in turn off his horse.

Once inside the office, with the door closed, Sheriff Dempster looked at Brogan and Pete in expectant silence. It was Brogan who spoke first.

'They robbed Pete of the money he was takin' to the miners,' he said. 'I just happened to come along at the right time.'

'An' just who the hell are you?' demanded Dempster.

'McNally, Brogan McNally,' said Brogan.

'Don't know the name,' said Dempster.

'Didn't expect you would,' said Brogan. 'First time I ever been in these parts.'

The sheriff sniffed disdainfully. 'An' the last, I hope.'

'I hope so too,' agreed Brogan.

'Right! So what's the story?'

'Like Brogan says,' said Pete. 'I was takin' the money up to the mines, like I usually do, when these four suddenly came at me.' He touched his bruised face. 'Beat me up an' then stole the money an' my mule. Just after, Brogan came along an' was bringin' me back to town when we came across 'em. We got the money back an' Esmerelda.'

'So what happened to Amos?' the sheriff grunted.

'Tried to pull a gun on me,' explained Brogan. 'I didn't have much choice but to shoot him.'

The sheriff turned to the three men. 'What you got to say?'

'They're lyin'!' asserted one. 'We was just restin' up, mindin' our own business when this saddle-bum suddenly opened up on us.'

'An' why should he do that?' asked Dempster.

'Who knows why a saddlebum does anythin'?'

'An' you say you didn't beat Pete up, or take the money?'

'What the hell we wanna do that for?'

'You tell me!' said Dempster. 'I don't see no reason why Pete should make up the story. Till I get to the bottom of it, you can all spend your time in the cell. I'll send out for Mr Mitchell, it was his money, I'll let him decide what to do.'

'An' me?' asked Brogan.

'You're free to go,' said Dempster. 'But this time I'm gonna make an exception to not havin' saddle tramps in town. You stay here until I've sorted things out.'

'I guess it makes a change from bein' hussled out!' Brogan grinned. 'I'll go stock up on some supplies.'

TWO

Sheriff Dempster followed Brogan and Pete Cummins out on to the street and was immediately besieged with questions from the crowd, which had grown while they were in the office. Dempster brushed aside the questions and ordered one of his deputies to take the body of Amos round to the undertaker. Seeing that they would get nothing from the sheriff, the crowd turned its attention on Brogan and Pete. Brogan too ignored everyone, but Pete, suddenly finding himself the centre of attraction, was beginning to relish the situation. Brogan simply smiled and left Pete to tell his story which, from what he heard, had acquired details not heard before.

Brogan's first call was to the general store where, as he had expected, the storekeeper seemed more interested in what had happened than in doing trade. Once again Brogan remained silent, browsing around the goods on display.

'Talkative, ain't you?' muttered the storekeeper.

'Ain't that much to talk about,' said Brogan.

'Ain't that much to talk about!' the storekeeper

exclaimed. 'You come into town carryin' a dead man, a man they reckon you killed, an' you say there ain't that much to talk about?'

'So I killed a man!' said Brogan. 'Ain't no big deal in that.'

The storekeeper looked Brogan up and down a little uneasily. 'Sounds like you do this sorta thing every day. Well let me tell you, Mister, this is a peaceful town, we ain't had a killin' here in the past four years, an' that was some guy who found another feller foolin' around with his wife.'

'Glad to hear it,' said Brogan, selecting a side of salt beef. 'Seems Sheriff Dempster does run a tight town.'

'Him an' Mr Mitchell,' agreed the storekeeper. 'What you kill Amos for?'

'Cos he was goin' to kill me,' replied Brogan, simply.

The storekeeper huffed and shuffled his feet. 'Good a reason as any, I suppose. I think you probably bought yourself a load of trouble though. Amos hadn't been workin' for Mr Mitchell all that long, but he'd made his mark, he was probably the best man Mr Mitchell had. They do say he was mighty handy with a gun, but that's only hearsay, he never had cause to prove it.'

'Seems to me,' Brogan laughed, 'the one time he needed to prove it, he failed. He sure won't have chance to prove it again.' He placed the salt beef on the counter and selected a small bag of flour and a bag of beans. 'That'll do for now. How much?'

'Six dollars fifty,' replied the storekeeper. Brogan handed him a ten-dollar bill. 'Three fifty change,' continued the storekeeper. 'Yeh, Amos was liked by Mr Mitchell an' by the others, 'specially those three you brought in. I'd hightail it outa here quick or I can see a lynchin' happenin'.'

'Lynchin' is against the law,' said Brogan. 'If this town is as tight as they say, neither Mitchell nor the sheriff is gonna stand by an' let it happen.'

'What they don't see they won't know about!' warned the storekeeper.

'They can try!' Brogan laughed. 'Thanks for the warnin' though.'

Brogan left the store and, as it was almost dusk, he led his horse along to the livery stable, followed by a small crowd of curious onlookers. The blacksmith did not seem at all surprised when Brogan asked if he too could bed down in the stable for the night.

'If the horses don't mind, I don't,' he said, with a wry smile. 'Cost you fifty cents though.'

'Fair enough,' agreed Brogan. 'How much for the horse?'

'Includin' feed, one dollar, in advance.'

Brogan paid up, unsaddled his horse and the blacksmith disappeared, not asking any questions, for which Brogan was quite thankful. Once he had settled his horse, he decided that a drink was the order of the day and went along to the nearest of the two saloons offered by Abbotsville. Before he could reach the saloon, however, Sheriff Dempster called from across the street.

'Mr Mitchell wants a word with you! He's in my office.'

Brogan shrugged, crossed the street and followed the sheriff the few yards to the office. A well dressed, rather plump man was standing with seeming impatience and showed obvious distaste at the sight of the man who had recovered his money.

'Yeh, you look an' smell like a saddlebum!' he growled. 'I suppose I gotta thank you for what you did?'

'Don't strain yourself!' Brogan laughed, lightly.

'Yeh! Well, thanks all the same,' said Mitchell. 'Don't understand you though. Most other fellers would've taken the money and got out while he could.'

'It warn't my money,' Brogan replied.

'Since when did things like that matter to a saddlebum?' Mitchell sneered.

'It matters to me,' replied Brogan.

'I guess it must. Sorry if I seem a little offhand, but I've long since learned nobody does nothin' for nothin'. What is it you want? I don't really believe you did it because you're a good citizen, 'specially since you're a stranger to these parts.'

'Peace an' quiet is all I want,' said Brogan.

'Peace and quiet! Well if that's all you want, you've sure got a funny way of gettin' it. Why didn't you just ignore it an' ride on? I know I would've.'

Brogan shrugged. 'Don't know really. I guess you could say I can't mind my own business.'

'It don't do to poke your nose in,' said Mitchell. 'Still, you did and I suppose I must be grateful to you. I must say I'm very surprised at those four, I thought I could trust them. Pete tells me they beat him up, took the money and his mule. Is that right?'

'Don't know what happened,' said Brogan. 'All I know is I came along an' found Pete lookin' pretty badly beaten. I've only got his word for what happened.'

'But it was you who found them!'

'Oh, sure, I found 'em,' Brogan admitted. 'They was countin' the money. That warn't the real reason I took 'em though. I could hear 'em talkin' an' they was goin' to wait for Pete an' kill him. I don't like things like that, 'specially since the old man was simply doin' his job.'

'Mmmm! That ties in with what Pete said,' said Mitchell. 'I wish there was some other way of gettin' the money to the mine, but I've tried other ways and they don't work. Pete seems to be the only man I can trust.'

'Then you've got a problem!' Brogan laughed.

'Since it isn't the money that seems to interest you, how would you like to do it?'

'I ain't that interested,' said Bogan. 'As long as I've got enough money for my needs, I'm happy.'

'Don't tell me you've got enough!' sneered Mitchell. 'I've never met a man yet who has enough, especially a man like you. I'm not sayin' that all men would steal, but they're always on the lookout for a quick dollar.'

'Then you just met one!' Brogan grinned. 'I don't care if you believe me or not, that's just the way things are.'

'I repeat my question. What do you expect out of this?'

'I reckon I deserve some sort of reward,' said Brogan. 'I hear that ten per cent is the usual.'

'Two hundred dollars!' Mitchell laughed, shaking his head. 'I can see you're not stupid. If you'd taken the money and tried to run, you knew there'd be a posse on your tail, so you decided that two hundred dollars earned legally was better than two thousand and being hounded.'

'Somethin' like that,' agreed Brogan.

'I'll have to think about it,' said Mitchell. 'Right, that's all for now, keep yourself available.'

'An' if I don't?'

'Then you probably save me two hundred dollars!'

'Logical!' Brogan grinned. 'I'll be around for a while. Now, since you don't want me no more, I'm goin' to the saloon an' have me a drink of beer.'

'There's hot baths in the barber's shop,' said Sheriff Dempster who, until that moment had kept a respectful silence.

'Bathin' ain't healthy,' said Brogan, looking darkly at the sheriff. 'I don't reckon I'll be payin' him a visit.'

Mitchell laughed. 'That figures. Where are you spendin' the night? Just in case I need to get hold of you.'

'In the livery stable,' replied Brogan.

'That figures too!' muttered Dempster. Brogan ignored him and went out on to the street.

The initial interest in him seemed to have died down, except for two small boys with a dog tied with a piece of rope around its neck. Brogan growled at them and they fled in terror, pulling the unwilling dog after them. He crossed the street and entered the saloon where the few customers eyed him warily, but made no comment. He ordered a beer and settled himself in a corner.

Meanwhile, Mitchell and the sheriff had gone through to the cells where they confronted the three men.

'So what the hell did you want to try a trick like that for?' demanded Mitchell. 'You must've known you'd get found out.'

The three men shrugged and looked at each other. 'It was Amos's idea,' said one. 'I don't know why we went along with it.'

'I'll tell you why, Jake!' Mitchell sneered. 'Because you all thought it was easy money. It was just too bad for you that saddle tramp came along. The question now is what to do with you. Personally I think you ought to stand trial. The only trouble with that is the circuit judge isn't due for another three months.' He turned to the sheriff. 'What do you think, Matt?'

'I could do without 'em clutterin' up my cells,' replied Dempster. 'If the judge was due soon it wouldn't be so bad, but I don't fancy keepin' 'em here for three months.'

'I agree,' said Mitchell. He looked hard at the three men. 'I think this is goin' to be your lucky day. If I decide to let you go, I want you out of this town straight away. Do you understand?' They looked truly amazed and nodded eagerly. 'That means you don't go back to the bunkhouse to collect anythin'. The moment you step outside this door, you get on your horses and ride out, and I never want to see your ugly faces again.'

'Sure thing, Mr Mitchell,' said Jake, nodding eagerly. 'An' thanks, we sure do appreciate it.'

'You'll appreciate the inside of this cell again if I so much as catch a smell of you in my territory,' snarled Dempster. 'Your guns are in the outer office an' your horses are in the livery.' He looked at Mitchell as he took the keys off a nearby hook and waited for the confirming nod before unlocking the cell. 'Now get outa here before we change our minds.'

In the outer office, Dempster handed them their guns, which they strapped on before walking, rather arrogantly, out into the street, where they suddenly gave a 'whoop' of delight and ran towards the livery.

Their exit from the sheriff's office had not gone unnoticed by Brogan and, somehow, he found that he was not too surprised. He had long since ceased to be surprised at the actions of some sheriffs and powerful property owners, but he did wonder if their release was the harbinger of more trouble. A couple of minutes later, Pete came breathlessly into the saloon, looked around and saw Brogan.

'They let 'em go!' he wheezed.

'I saw!' said Brogan.

'What the hell they want to do a thing like that for? It don't make sense, they ought to stand trial.'

'I guess they figured it warn't worth the bother,' said Brogan.

'I don't like it,' said Pete, sitting alongside Brogan. 'Mr Mitchell just told me I gotta try an' get that money out to the mine again, in the mornin'.'

'Are you?'

'I oughta say I won't,' said Pete. 'But if I refuse, he's made it plain it'll be the last time he'll use me, an' I can't afford to lose this job.'

'Then I guess you got a problem. Me, I'd tell him to stuff the job. In fact I've already refused to take it on.'

'He asked you?' Pete sighed. 'I can't say as I'm surprised.'

'So what you gonna do?' Brogan asked.

'Do it, I guess.' He sighed again. 'It looks like I got no choice, not if I wanna earn some money.'

'We all gotta live,' observed Brogan. 'I ain't never worked for nobody, not by choice anyhow, an' I get by.'

'If'n I was a few years younger, I reckon I'd do the same as you,' said Pete. 'But I'm too old now, I gotta take what I can get, when I can get it.'

'He's comin' over,' said Brogan, peering above the frosted glass of the large window. 'Maybe we'll find out why he let 'em go.'

A minute later, Mitchell came in, looked briefly

around and strode over to them. 'I guess there's no
need to tell you I've let them go,' he said, grinning
slightly.

'We saw!' said Brogan. 'Seems kinda crazy to me,
but I guess it's none of my business what you do.'

'That's right,' said Mitchell. 'It ain't none of your
business. I just came in to see if you've changed
your mind about workin' for me. I can pay twenty
dollars a trip and I could probably find plenty of
other work for you, five dollars a week and all
found.'

'No thanks,' said Brogan. 'I was just sayin' I ain't
never done paid work for nobody in my life, 'ceptin'
escortin' a few folk here an' there sometimes.'

'I thought you might say that,' said Mitchell. 'It's
a pity, but I'm not goin' to argue with you. Now,
about that reward you're tryin' to claim. I've given
it some thought and I suppose I do owe you
somethin', but you're not goin' to earn it quite so
simple as that. I'll pay you the two hundred,
providin' you travel with Pete an' take that money
out to the mine. This is special, most of the money
is bonus, normally Pete doesn't carry more than
about five or six hundred. I can't afford to lose this
lot and if I don't get it out to the miners, they'll
down tools.'

'The miners downin' tools ain't no problem that
concerns me,' said Brogan.

Mitchell laughed. 'There, I've got to agree with
you, which is why I'll only pay you the two hundred
if you'll do it.'

'I reckon I can get by without the money,' said

Brogan. 'I wasn't expectin' any when I headed this way, so I ain't exactly lost anythin'.'

'You'd never make a businessman,' said Mitchell. 'To be successful you've got to grab every opportunity that comes along to make money.'

'I ain't never claimed to be a businessman,' replied Brogan, simply. 'I ain't never had the urge.'

'So you're quite content to ride out without any reward?'

'Yeh, never seen the sense in bustin' a gut to earn a dollar.'

'Maybe you've got a point,' mused Mitchell. 'It looks like you're on your own, Pete.'

'I can manage!' muttered Pete.

'I don't know why you let them three go,' said Brogan. 'But don't you think that was kinda stupid? They'll know you've got to get that money out, so what's to stop 'em takin' it again?' As he spoke, the three men raced along the street on their horses. 'I'd say they was headin' out to the hills. All they gotta do is hole up an' wait.'

'Never thought of that,' admitted Mitchell.

'You may be a good businessman,' Brogan laughed, 'but you sure don't seem to know nothin' 'bout men. They probably thought you was crazy to let 'em go an' if I know anythin' they'll wait up somewheres, take the money an' laugh at you.'

'So that makes it another reason why I need you to go with Pete,' said Mitchell. 'You seem to be able to handle yourself, they won't be too keen to take you on.'

'You know them hills,' said Pete. 'A whole army could lie up there an' not be seen till you was in the middle of 'em.'

'And nobody knows those hills like you do,' said Mitchell. 'You've avoided the regular bandits most of the time. You could quite easily find another way through. Those three will be waiting on the usual trail, they're not bright enough to realise there are other ways through.'

'If you're so worried about the money,' said Brogan. 'Why don't you send out some of your other boys with Pete?'

Mitchell laughed loudly, making everyone in the saloon look at them. 'That's easy! I wouldn't trust any of them with that much money. Pete's probably already told you that I've tried that a couple of times.'

'Yeh, he told me!' said Brogan. 'So why not go with them yourself?'

'Because I'm a business man, not a gunman,' said Mitchell. 'I pay other people to do things like that for me.'

'It'd seem more business-like if you was to go with him,' observed Brogan. 'At least you'd be sure of it gettin' through.'

'I'd probably get myself killed,' said Mitchell. 'I'm not prepared to take that chance.'

'Don't you ever go up to the mines then?'

'I have to, sometimes,' admitted Mitchell. 'But I never carry any money with me, an' those bandits know that.'

'Yeh, them bandits!' said Brogan. 'Just who are

they?'

'A bunch of half-breeds from what I can gather. Pete knows more about them than I do, ask him.'

'Mostly half-breeds,' said Pete. 'One full blooded Indian an' two whites are with 'em though.'

'How many?' asked Brogan

'Eight, I think,' said Pete. 'Don't know for sure.'

'Hasn't anybody tried to flush 'em out?' asked Brogan.

'We tried it a couple of times,' said Mitchell. 'But you must've seen what it's like up there. Like Pete says, a whole army could hide out an' not be found.'

'So you just let 'em rob Pete whenever they feel like it?'

'I don't have much choice,' said Mitchell, with a wry grin. 'If there was a way you could be sure I'd take it.'

Brogan shrugged. 'It's your problem, not mine.'

'And I stick by what I said,' said Mitchell. 'I'll pay you the two hundred, providin' you get Pete through safely.'

'Don't see why I should stick my neck out,' replied Brogan. 'I'm darned sure nobody would bother about me.'

'That's for sure!' Mitchell laughed. 'Think about it though. I'm quite sure you could do with the money. I'll leave you and Pete to talk about it.' With that, he left them.

'Don't blame you for not wantin' to go,' said Pete, as he watched Mitchell leave. 'For my part though, I'd sure appreciate it if you was to ride with me. The way you knew where Amos an' his cronies were tells me we'd get through.'

Two other men had been lounging against the bar and quite obviously they had heard everything that had been said. They both turned slowly and sneered at Brogan.

'I'll tell you why he won't do it!' said the taller of the two, laughing. "'Cos he's nothin' but a cowardly saddlebum! All saddlebums is shit scared; I know, I met quite a few.'

'You ain't met this one!' said Brogan, very quietly.

'We can smell you though!' came the response. 'You smell a whole lot worse'n any other we ever met. What you do, fall in a cesspit?'

Brogan chose to ignore them, turning his back on them. This seemed to annoy them.

'No saddlebum ever turned his back on us!' the other man rasped. 'Not unless he was runnin' scared! You runnin' scared, bum?'

'I ain't run scared from nobody!' said Brogan, again quietly.

'Watch 'em!' whispered Pete. 'They is another two of Mitchell's men. He uses them as troubleshooters.'

Brogan sighed deeply and stood up, turning slowly to face them. He had not wanted this, but he realized that a showdown was inevitable.

'That's right!' the taller man hissed. 'Get outa this town while you can. We don't like stinkin' saddlebums here, 'specially one what killed a friend of ours.'

'He asked for it,' said Brogan. 'I suppose it don't matter none that they were goin' to kill Pete here?'

'Nobody gives a damn about an old man like him!'

'I do!'

'An' nobody gives a damn about you either! Now run, like the coward you are.'

'Or what?'

'Or this!'

Neither man had even drawn their gun when they found themselves staring into the barrel of Brogan's Colt. A gasp went up from the rest of the occupants of the saloon and there was the sound of people diving for cover.

'Your move!' invited Brogan.

Both men stared at the gun in Brogan's hand and then at each other. Very slowly, their guns slipped back into their holsters. 'You got lucky, that's all,' said the taller one.

'I guess I spent all my life gettin' lucky,' said Brogan. 'I must be gettin' soft in my old age, any other time you'd both be lyin' on the floor nursin' holes in your heads.'

'OK, Mister,' said the other. 'You made your point. You're fast. You'd better keep one eye behind you through.'

Brogan laughed. 'Ask Pete, he knows I got eyes up my arse!'

The two men stormed out of the saloon, swearing loudly and Brogan returned to his drink and Pete.

THREE

'Keep your ears open, old girl,' Brogan said to his horse, as he bedded down for the night. 'It's my guess we're gonna have some visitors.' His horse snorted and nodded her head and looked at him with wide eyes. 'An' don't you go lookin' at me like that,' he continued. 'I didn't invite no trouble.' She snorted, as if not believing him. 'OK, so maybe I did. I shouldn't've come into town. It's allus the same, towns almost always spell trouble. Dunno why it should be, but that's the way it seems to happen.' The horse nodded knowingly.

To a casual observer, it would have appeared that the prospect of trouble did not seem to have any effect on Brogan's ability to sleep easily, but years of conditioning had given him the ability to both sleep and listen for sounds which did not belong to wherever he was. For more than four hours nothing happened but, just after two o'clock, the door of the livery stable very slowly opened and two shadows eased themselves through the narrow gap.

The dark shapes stood for a moment or two

surveying the various horses and eventually one of the shapes nudged the other and pointed at Brogan's horse. Alongside her, on a bed of straw, they could see their quarry, still asleep under a blanket and they moved stealthily towards it, each clasping a knife.

'Nobody makes a fool outa us!' rasped one. 'Least of all some dirty old saddlebum!' His knife plunged downwards, to be quickly followed by the other man embedding his knife into the sleeping form. Both men stabbed three or four times more.

'You just killed my bedroll!' hissed a voice from somewhere behind them. Both men turned and stared into the darkness in disbelief, their arms poised in mid-strike.

'Bastard!' growled one. Suddenly they were both drawing their guns, but two shots ensured that they never fired them.

The reaction of the townsfolk was remarkably quick. Within two minutes the stable door was crashing open and four men, headed by the sheriff, burst in. One of them was carrying a flaming torch and they very soon discovered the two men slumped in the straw.

'What the hell's goin' on?' demanded Sheriff Dempster. 'Where are you, McNally?'

'Right behind you,' came Brogan's voice. The three men with the sheriff swung round, their guns aimed in the direction the voice came from. 'Tell 'em to take it easy,' Brogan ordered. 'I'd hate to have to kill innocent men.'

'Cool it!' said Dempster. They lowered their guns. 'Come on out, McNally, where we can see you. You've got some explainin' to do.'

Brogan very slowly came into the light of the torch, his gun still at the ready. 'Obvious ain't it?' he said.

Just then, there was a groan from one of the bodies and the sheriff bent down to examine him. 'He ain't dead!' he cried. 'Sam, you go get the doc here on the double!' Sam did as he was ordered. An examination of the other man showed that he was also still alive. 'Looks like you're lucky, McNally. If they'd been dead I'd've run you in for murder.'

'Murder?' queried Brogan. 'I suppose it don't count that they just tried to kill me?' He pointed at the knives nearby and at his bedroll. 'They didn't hurt me, but they sure didn't do my roll no good. Call it what you like, Sheriff, but what I did was in self-defence.'

Sheriff Dempster sighed. 'Yeh, I heard what you did in the saloon. These two are supposed to be pretty fast on the draw, but accordin' to what I heard you made 'em look like some fumblin' kids. I guess they didn't like that.'

'I thought you were supposed to run a tight town?' said Brogan. 'More'n four years since you had a killin'.'

'Yeh!' Dempster grunted, standing up. 'More'n four years an' suddenly you drift into town.'

'I've only killed one,' Brogan reminded, 'an' even you gotta admit that was in a fair fight.'

'That's what makes it so darned annoyin',' said Dempster, with a wry laugh. 'These two as well! I gotta admit it looks like you did what you did in self-defence. Why this town, McNally? What've we done to deserve you?'

'You just got lucky!' Brogan laughed.

Their banter was interrupted by the arrival of Sam with the doctor, who immediately bent down to examine the injured men. He cursed and ordered the torch to be brought nearer.

'They'll live!' the doc finally declared. 'Gut wounds, messy, but I don't think there's any real damage. Get them over to my office, I got me some diggin' an' stitchin' to do.' He looked up at Brogan. 'You did this, I suppose?' Brogan nodded. 'I heard there was a troublemaker in town. It makes a change from dealin' with stomach pains an' boils I suppose, but I can do without this kind of business any day.'

'Sorry you had to be called out in the middle of the night,' said Brogan. 'But you can blame them for that, it was their idea, not mine.'

'I reckon the whole town knows how you made them look small in the saloon,' said the doc. 'I suppose they had it comin' to them. They've got far too used to throwin' their weight around. Maybe it's a good thing an' maybe it's not. All I can say is I hope you don't stay around too long, for your sake as well as mine. I don't want this kind of business an' I'd sure hate to have to be diggin' a bullet out of you.'

'That goes for me too,' said Dempster. 'In less

than one day you've given me more trouble than I've had in the ten years I've been doin' this job.'

'It was you who told me not to leave town,' Brogan reminded.

'Yeh, well, I just changed my mind!' muttered the sheriff. 'You can go as soon as you like an' the sooner the better.'

'I'll be on my way in the mornin',' Brogan promised.

Two rough stretchers were made to carry the injured men down the street to the doc's office, a street now alive with inquisitive people. From the comments Brogan could hear from the livery stable door, it did not appear that too many of them were bothered about the men. Comments such as 'It serves 'em right!' and 'They had it comin' to 'em!' could be plainly heard.

'I'm just curious,' said Sheriff Dempster to Brogan. 'It was pretty dark in there. Did you shoot to kill?'

'Like you say,' replied Brogan, 'it was pretty dark. All I can say is they is darned lucky it was dark. If it had been light, it'd be the undertaker who was takin' 'em now, not the doc.'

'I guess so!' the sheriff sighed. 'The quicker you're out of town the better.' He did not give Brogan the opportunity to reply and ran after the doc.

Brogan shook his head and went back inside the stable. 'I guess that's about all the excitement we're gonna get tonight,' he said to his horse. 'You can sleep easy now.' She snorted, rather contemptuously. 'I mean it! I don't reckon anyone else is gonna try nothin' tonight.' He too settled down, easy in his own mind.

'McNally, I want a word with you!' The order came from Seth Mitchell. 'You just put two of my best men out of action.'

'If they was your best, I'd start to worry!' Brogan laughed.

'All right, so they're not as handy as you are with a gun. That's what I want to talk to you about.'

'If you're figurin' to offer me a job, I already told you, I don't work for nobody, never have an' never will. Not regular anyhow.'

'I'm not offerin' you a job,' replied Mitchell, coming over to Brogan. 'All I'm askin' you to do is go with Pete an' get that money through safely. I suppose by rights I still owe you two hundred, but I don't intend to pay it unless you earn it.'

'Accordin' to my reckonin', I already earned it!'

'Maybe you have,' Mitchell said, 'but I don't reckon you'll be able to find anyone in these parts who will enforce it.'

'I ain't even gonna try,' said Brogan. 'Anyhow, I reckon it'd be another twenty if I was to do it.'

'Another twenty! How do you make that out?'

'Two hundred reward money an', by your own admission, another twenty you'd pay for any man doin' the job.'

Mitchell laughed. 'I'd say you were in no position to bargain.'

'Better position than you,' said Brogan. 'I can manage without the money but you can't afford not to get the payroll through.'

Again Mitchell laughed. 'Maybe you're not such a bad business man at that. OK, you've got it, if that's what you want. I'll tell you what, I'll make it up to two hundred an' fifty.'

Brogan thought for a moment. In truth, he needed more cash, he had counted his money that morning and was rather dismayed to find that the sum total of his worth was only eight dollars and twenty-two cents. He had been worse off in the past, but not that often, and there was no way of knowing when he would be in the position of gathering himself a few dollars again. It was this thought and this thought only which made him waver.

'The sheriff wants me outa town,' he said. 'It ain't often I argue with sheriffs.'

'Dempster will do as he's told,' assured Mitchell. 'Just like everyone else in this territory.'

''Ceptin' them bandits!'

'I wouldn't need the likes of you if it wasn't for them,' said Mitchell. 'Well, what do you say?'

'I gotta think about it,' said Brogan. 'Where's Pete? I reckon I'd better talk to him.'

'Probably still in his bed,' sneered Mitchell. 'It isn't often he sees the light of day before eight.'

'I'll go talk to him. Where is he?'

Mitchell pointed down the street. 'The shack next to the old church is his place.' He laughed loudly. 'You'll feel at home there. From what I can gather it smells worse than a pigsty.'

Brogan ignored the remark. 'I'll let you know in an hour. Where can I find you?'

'My office. That's over the bank.'

'You own the bank too?'

'Unfortunately, no,' said Mitchell. 'I own almost everything else, but not the bank.'

'Nice to know some things stay the same,' said Brogan. 'I'll go talk to Pete an' let you know.'

Mitchell could hardly control his smile. He knew very well that Brogan would agree to do the job and left him to return his horse to the stable.

Brogan walked slowly along the street, conscious of the gazes and whispers which followed his progress, and began to wonder just how popular Seth Mitchell really was, but he dismissed the thought, deciding that Mitchell's popularity was the least of his concerns.

As Mitchell had predicted, Pete was still in bed and, again as Mitchell had predicted, the shack did smell worse than a pigsty. Pete dressed only in faded, red longjohns, which looked as through they had not been changed for many months, opened the door with bleary eyes.

'Brogan!' He yawned and scratched himself. 'Come on in. Don't mind the mess, I ain't had time to tidy up yet.' It looked as if Pete never found the time to tidy up. 'What can I do for you?'

'Mitchell asked me to go with you,' he said, stepping inside the litter strewn, single room that served as home for Pete Cummins.

'I already know that,' said Pete, giving another

gaping yawn. 'I know you also said you wouldn't do it.' He pulled open the tattered sack that hung across the only window. 'That's better, I can see what I'm doin' now.' He looked hard at Brogan and smiled slightly. 'I may not be too bright, but the fact you're here talkin' about it tells me that you've changed your mind.'

'I'm thinkin' about it,' admitted Brogan.

'I'd say you've thought about it!' Pete laughed and reached among the litter on the floor for a bottle, from which he took a long drink. 'Aah! That's better!' He smacked his lips and wiped the neck of the bottle on his dirty sleeve. 'Drink?' he said, offering the bottle to Brogan. 'Whisky! It ain't the best, but it sure gets the circulation goin'.'

'No thanks,' Brogan declined. 'I ain't a whisky drinker, 'specially not at this hour of the day.'

Pete shrugged. 'Any hour of the day is a good time for whisky. So what made you change your mind?'

'Money!' said Brogan. 'Money an' the fact that I ain't got enough of it right now. Even a feller like me's gotta have some cash in his pocket an' since it ain't my habit to steal it, I guess I gotta earn it while I can.'

'Yeh, money talks sense to any man,' said Pete, with a knowing grin. He tapped the bottle. 'A man's gotta have money for the little comforts in life.'

'I don't need them kinda comforts,' said Brogan. 'I still need to get by though.'

'So Mitchell won't come up with the ten per cent that's rightly yours,' said Pete. 'Can't say as I'm surprised.'

'He says if I want it I gotta earn it.'

'That figures too. OK, so what do you want me to do? Don't get me wrong, it'll be a pleasure havin' you along, I'll feel a whole lot safer.' He took another draw on the bottle. 'Sure you won't have some?' Brogan shook his head. 'Suit yourself! I reckon you can expect trouble from them two you had the drop on in the saloon last night, 'specially if you stay in town.'

'You mean you ain't heard?' asked Brogan, rather surprised. He thought that everyone in town knew.

'Heard what?'

'They won't be no trouble to anyone for a good while, they got their own problems. Last I heard the doc was sortin' 'em out for 'em. You musta heard the commotion last night?'

'Didn't hear nothin',' assured Pete. 'What's been goin' on?'

Brogan laughed. 'You must be about the only person in Abbotsville what didn't hear. They tried to kill me last night. Tried to stab me to death in the livery.'

'I can see they didn't succeed!' Pete laughed and took another drink. 'I take it you didn't kill 'em. Might've been better if'n you had.'

'They was lucky. It was dark.'

'I bet Mitchell is mighty sore about it,' said Pete. 'That's three of his best men you've taken out, an' another three who've been sent packin'.'

'I don't give a shit how sore Mitchell feels,' said Brogan. 'He needs me now an' he knows I could do with the money.'

'Always did have an eye for business!' Pete laughed. 'So join the club, Brogan! You just sold your soul to the devil.'

'For one job only!' asserted Brogan.

'So you say!' Pete laughed again. 'We'll see!'

'This one job!' Brogan asserted again. 'I didn't come here to tell you about my problems though. What I want to know is, how far is it to this mine?'

'On a good horse, with no problems an' fine weather, a full day's ride. On my old mule an' that old nag of yours an' takin' into account we're sure to meet trouble, at least two days, maybe three, if we make it at all.'

'I don't reckon them bandits will be all that much trouble.'

'It ain't them I'm thinkin' about,' said Pete. 'I'm thinkin' about them three that Mitchell let off yesterday. They got nothin' to lose now. I reckon they is sure to try an' take the payroll an' killin' you will be an added bonus for 'em.'

'An' you're still prepared to go through with it, knowin' they'll be up there?'

'I sold my soul to the devil a long time ago,' said Pete, rather sadly. 'If I wanna be able to buy my comfort … ' He tapped the bottle. 'Then I gotta do as I'm told.'

'An' supposin' you get killed?'

Pete laughed. 'Then I sure won't be needin' no

earthly comforts! Dead men don't have no use for money.'

Brogan was forced to smile. The dirty old man standing almost obscenely in front of him, echoed his own thoughts exactly. 'What do they dig out up there, gold?'

'Nothin' so grand as that!' said Pete. 'Lead, nothin' but lead! They find some silver too, lead an' silver often get found together, but it's mainly lead.'

'Lead! What does Mitchell want lead for?'

'Your bullets is made of lead,' said Pete. 'An' a whole host of other things. Lead is more useful than gold. He sells it all over the place. One of his biggest customers is the army, for bullets I guess, but he does sell it to other folk.'

'I guess he knows his own business,' said Brogan. 'Two days! I guess I can stand that. I'll go tell Mitchell I'll do the job. What time you startin'?'

'Just as soon as I'm dressed,' said Pete. 'I pick up the payroll from the bank.'

'I'll meet you outside,' said Brogan. He left the stench of Pete's shack and wandered back along the street to the bank. There was no need to go up to Mitchell's office, he was standing outside talking to the sheriff.

'Well?' asked Mitchell, as Brogan approached.

'I reckon you already know the answer to that,' said Brogan.

'I knew you'd do it!' declared Mitchell, with a wry laugh. 'I told you he would, didn't I, Matt?' he said to the sheriff.

Matt Dempster grunted. 'I guess you do have your uses after all. Personally I'd rather see you leavin' town permanently.'

'Could be it is permanent,' said Brogan. 'We might both of us get killed, or maybe I'll just take off with the money.'

'I don't reckon you'll do that,' said Mitchell. 'If that's what you wanted you'd've done it while you had the chance. No, I don't reckon you want your face on any wanted poster.'

'It ain't never been on one up to now,' said Brogan. 'I guess I'm too old to start now.'

'For Mr Mitchell's sake, I hope you get through,' said Dempster. 'As for the chance you might get killed, I can't say as I, or anyone else, are goin' to shed too many tears over that.'

'No,' agreed Mitchell. 'I'll be honest and say I don't really care what happens to you. All I want you to do is make sure that payroll gets through.'

'An' all I want is what's rightfully mine,' said Brogan. 'Just make sure you keep to your side of the bargain, that's all.'

'I've never reneged on a deal yet,' said Mitchell, puffing his chest out slightly. 'If I make a promise, I keep to it.'

'Then we've got a deal,' said Brogan. 'I said I'd meet Pete outside the bank.'

'Bank don't open till nine,' said the sheriff. 'Mr Evans, the bank president, is a stickler for doin' things right.'

'Matt'll see to it all,' said Mitchell. 'I've got some more business to see to right now. I wish you good

luck, Mr McNally, but somehow I don't think
you're goin' to need it.' With that he left and
returned to his office.

'How about you, Sheriff?' asked Brogan. 'Do you
reckon I'm gonna need any luck?'

'I reckon that as long as you've got a gun handy,
luck don't play much part of your calculations,'
replied Dempster. 'I meant what I said when I
said I wouldn't shed no tears if you get killed, but
I got me this strange feelin' you'll turn up here,
demandin' your money again. Just like a lump of
dogshit stuck to a boot, you never seem to get it
all off.'

'Best way of gettin' rid of the shit is to get rid of
the dog,' said Brogan. 'Don't worry 'bout me,
Sheriff. Just make sure Mitchell pays up an' I'll be
on my way, for good.'

'Yeh, I reckon you will,' said Dempster, grinning
slightly. 'Most dogs don't foul the same place
twice.'

'Not unless they is penned in!' Brogan laughed.
'Just don't try pennin' me up. I know Mitchell
would like me to work for him, but I think both
you an' I wouldn't like it.'

'I'll make sure he forgets the idea,' assured the
sheriff.

With over an hour to go before the bank opened,
Brogan returned to the stable to collect his horse
and led it back to the bank, where he lounged on
the boardwalk until it was time. The sight of him
made various of the citizens of Abbotsville decide
that they suddenly had business on the other side

of the street. One woman, with a protesting child in tow, dragged the erring offspring across the street with threats of letting the bogey man get him if he did not behave himself. To the boy's credit, Brogan thought, he turned when they were halfway across and stuck his tongue out at him. Brogan gave a low growl and the boy quickly hid behind his mother's skirts.

At about two minutes to nine, a carriage drew up and a well dressed man got out, instructing the driver to be back at lunch time. He looked distastefully at Brogan, but said nothing and unlocked the bank. At almost the same time, Pete and the sheriff arrived.

'I've been meanin' to ask, Sheriff,' said Brogan. 'How goes it with them two I shot last night?'

'They'll live,' muttered Dempster. 'No thanks to you though.'

'Wish I'd been there,' said Pete.

'You were probably too full of whisky to notice anythin',' said Dempster sourly. 'I can never understand why Mr Mitchell trusts you with the job.'

'I'm the only one that'll do it,' said Pete. 'He knows I ain't about to make off with the money.'

The sheriff grunted and nodded them into the bank, where they were met by the doleful face of the president, Mr Evans. He looked questioningly at Dempster, who assured him that everything was all right. He made no comment and handed over a satchel to Pete.

'Ain't you gonna check it?' asked Brogan.

'What for?' said Pete. 'I don't ask what's in there, I only see that it gets delivered.'

'You could help yourself to some of it,' Brogan pointed out.

'There's a seal on it!' Seth Mitchell's voice boomed from behind. He came forward and took the satchel off Pete and showed Brogan the seal. 'If this seal is broken, they'll know it's been tampered with.'

Brogan looked at the satchel and decided that he could easily get the money out without breaking the seal, but he shrugged and said nothing. It was no business of his. They walked out on to the street, leaving Sheriff Dempster in the bank and walked toward their horses.

'There's a couple of bottles of whisky in my office,' said Mitchell. 'I know you like a drop, Pete. Do you like whisky, McNally?'

'Not usually,' said Brogan, as Pete scuttled off to Mitchell's office.

'I'd better make sure he don't take the best Scotch!' Mitchell suddenly grinned and raced off to his office. A short time later both men returned and a short time after that Pete and Brogan were riding slowly out of town. Brogan was beginning to have second thoughts, but decided that it was too late now.

FOUR

'I been thinkin',' said Brogan after they had been travelling for about half an hour. 'If there is anyone waitin' for you, they'll be lyin' up somewhere along the trail you usually take. We oughta go some other way.'

'There ain't much choice,' said Pete. 'Leastways not at first. This is the only trail, I know, I've tried to find other ways. Either the hills are too darned steep or they're so thickly wooded it's almost inpossible to get through. This way is bad enough, but at least it's possible.'

'Not at first!' said Brogan. 'You mean there are other ways later on?'

'Sure, there's other ways,' nodded Pete, 'but they ain't easy an' I reckon them half-breeds know most of 'em by now.'

'I wasn't thinkin' of them, I was thinkin' of them other three.'

'Don't suppose they know,' agreed Pete. 'Trouble is there ain't no other ways until after where you found me.'

Brogan laughed. 'I'm pretty certain those three

are goin' to make a try at grabbin' this payroll, they ain't got nothin' to lose now, but I also reckon havin' the bandits lookin' for it too is goin' to be to our advantage.'

'Two lots of crazy robbers up there an' you reckon it's goin' to be to our advantage? I know I'm a bit thick in the head, but it strikes me that one lot is bad enough, so two lots must be twice as bad. I don't follow you.'

'Simple!' Brogan smiled. 'As I see it, it ain't at all likely that they'll be workin' together. I'll bet that even now them half-breeds have got 'em spotted. Maybe they've even taken them. If they have, it'll sure save us a lot of trouble.'

'Maybe they have,' agreed Pete, 'but I still don't see how that helps us in any way.'

'Well, let's assume that they haven't taken 'em. Do you suppose for one moment that they is gonna allow three strangers to their territory just ride in an' take the money?'

'No, I gotta agree with that.'

'An' from the half-breeds' point of view, do they wait until them three have taken the money an' then take it off them? I don't think so. It's far easier for them to try an' take it from one old man an' one old saddlebum than off three well armed men.'

'It'd make more sense to take it off us,' agreed Pete.

'Exactly!' Brogan grinned. 'So already both sets have got a problem, they've gotta keep a sharp look out behind 'em.'

'So how does that help us?'

'Dunno, yet,' said Brogan. 'It's just that I like to know what the opposition is up against. I'll think of somethin'.'

'Still don't see how it's gonna help us. Dead is dead, no matter who pulls the trigger.'

They were now approaching the foothills and Brogan's senses were on full alert, looking and listening for any minute but tell-tale signs of anything that did not belong.

They wound their way along the narrow, twisting trail, catching glimpses of Abbotsville far below. To the right of them the rock rose almost sheer and treeless and to their left it fell, again almost sheer, into a deep ravine, perhaps a hundred feet deep. Of all the places an ambush could take place, Brogan thought that this spot was the most unlikely. If either party did try and ambush them at that point, there was a very good chance that the satchel containing the money would be lost in the ravine.

As he thought, there was no sign of anyone and half an hour later they were at the top where the ground dipped slightly. From here onwards ambush could come at any time and Brogan was once again fully alert.

'Hole up here!' Brogan instructed Pete. 'I'm goin' on ahead to see if I can see anythin' or anyone. See that ridge up ahead?' Pete nodded. 'I'll give you a signal from there if it's all clear.'

'An' if you don't?' asked Pete.

'Then I reckon you'll hear shootin'. If I still don't

give the signal from that ridge you is on your own,
I'll likely as not be dead.'

'Can't say fairer'n that,' agreed Pete.

Brogan rode on, very slowly, listening and
looking. He passed the place where he had
discovered Pete and was reasonably satisfied that
there was no-one waiting in ambush. His one brief
scare came when he disturbed a small herd of
deer, but having disturbed the animals, he was
even more certain that there was nobody. Had
there been, it was most unlikely that the deer
would have stopped around. The ridge was
reached without difficulty and from it, he had a
good view of the trail ahead. Again, there were
none of the tell-tale signs he was looking for.

'So far so good!' he said to himself.

'Maybe it is,' he replied. He usually talked to
himself or his horse. 'But you is forgettin' one
thing.'

'An' what's that?'

'Indians an' half-breeds! They ain't like your
usual white feller. To most whites, all that out
there is just a bunch of trees an' things, most
wouldn't know how to hide up properly. Indians
though, they is different. If they is used to this
kinda country they know how to use it.'

'Yeh, which means they'll also be able to detect
me even if the others can't. I was forgettin' that.'

'Personally I reckon you was quite mad to agree
to this. I know we need the money, but we've
managed before, we could manage again.'

'Too late now,' he replied. 'We can't just up an'

leave Pete.'

'Too soft, that's your trouble.'

'Yeh!' he agreed.

Having sorted himself, he rode into full view where he knew Pete would see him and waved. There was an answering wave and he could see Pete leading his mule out of the cover of a bush, mount up and slowly plod towards him. It seemed an eternity before Pete was alongside, puffing and wheezing as though he had walked the whole way himself.

'I need a drink!' puffed Pete, taking one of his comforts from his saddle-bag. 'Want some?'

'No thanks,' said Brogan. 'Whisky ain't no good to a man out here, 'ceptin' to keep the cold out. It dulls the senses.'

Pete took a long drink, coughed and spluttered and then smacked his lips before wiping them on his sleeve. 'That's better! I guess you're right about it dullin' the senses, but I reckon my senses got dulled a long time ago.'

'Probably,' agreed Brogan. 'I been thinkin' 'bout them Indians, 'specially the full blooded ones. Are they from these parts?'

'Born an' bred,' Pete confirmed. 'Rest of the tribe ain't no bother, but for some reason they teamed up with the half-breeds an' the two white fellers. I hear tell they was thrown out of the tribe 'cos they was nothin' but troublemakers. Indians is strange like that. If one of their kind don't conform, they kick him out.'

'At least they usually look after their own,' said

Brogan. 'Where'd the whites an' the half-breeds come from?'

'That's anybody's guess,' said Pete. 'More'n like the half-breeds is the leftovers from the time when there was a big army post near here. Half-breeds is despised by both whites an' Indians. The whites too is probably from the army days. Who knows?'

'OK, now you hole up here while I go on ahead. I'll give you the signal from that big rock up ahead.'

'Are we gonna go on like this all the way?' asked Pete. 'At this rate it'll take up more'n three days.'

'Better to take three days an' get there alive than one day an' end up dead,' said Brogan. 'You wanted my help, so you gotta play it my way.'

'I ain't arguin',' said Pete. 'Only trouble is I ain't got enough whisky to last three days.'

'Do you good to go without!' Brogan laughed.

Once again Brogan rode slowly ahead and once again he neither saw nor heard anything which might be men lying in ambush. He climbed the rock and signalled to Pete and again waited for him to join him. This time Pete did not reach for his comfort bottle, grinning sheepishly and admitting that he could probably do without it, this time at least.

This operation of Brogan scouting ahead and Pete following was repeated half a dozen times more and even Brogan was beginning to believe that he might just be too over-cautious. The effect of it all was to slow their rate of travel down to such an extent that Brogan reckoned they had only travelled about twelve miles in the day. Just before dusk he found a safe place to camp but he refused to let Pete light a fire.

'No fire!' Pete grumbled. 'Why not? There ain't nobody gonna see nothin'! I know you wanna get through with no trouble, but I think not havin' a fire is goin' too far.'

'You think so, do you?' said Brogan. 'There won't be no moon tonight, so any light'll stand out like a beacon.'

'Even in these trees?'

'Even in these trees!' replied Brogan. 'If you wanna get yourself warm you'll have to take some of that comfort you brought with you.'

'Darned good job I've got three bottles with me!' muttered Pete, but he did not argue further. He took the half-full bottle out of his saddle-bag and drew the cork with his teeth. 'Want a swig?'

'No thanks,' said Brogan. 'I'm gonna do a bit of scoutin' around.'

'What for? There ain't nothin' to see.'

'More than you think!' Brogan grinned. 'I don't reckon either the Indians or those other three will even think that they might be seen, so I reckon they is bound to have fires. If they is anywhere about, I'll spot 'em.'

'An' they won't be out lookin' for nobody either,' Pete pointed out. 'Not if they got any sense that is.'

'I don't reckon they will either,' agreed Brogan, 'but no fire.'

'OK, OK, you're the boss!' grumbled Pete. 'Still seems that you is bein' too cautious though.'

'Bein' cautious has kept me alive this long,' said Brogan. 'An' I intend to stay alive.'

They had to content themselves with dry bread and some cheese that Pete had brought along for their supper, not that either of them had any complaints about that, Brogan had had to go without anything to eat for long periods before now. Pete, however, continued to grumble for the next two hours.

'I'm goin'!' announced Brogan, deciding that he'd had enough of Pete and his grumblings. 'I don't know how long I'll be, it all depends on what I find.'

'I won't wait up for you,' Pete grunted. 'If you ain't back by dawn I'll assume you ain't comin' back an' start off on my own.'

'You do just that,' agreed Brogan. 'I should be back well before then though, I ain't gonna look too far.'

This time Brogan left his horse and disappeared into the darkness on foot. At first he followed the trail, reasoning that if there was anyone camped up for the night, they would not be too far off the trail.

His progress was slow and painstaking for the next hour and he neither saw nor heard anything other than the normal night sounds of thickly wooded countryside. It was when he was standing on top of a small ridge that the first signs of anything out of the ordinary came to him.

It was faint, very faint, but his keen ears detected the uneasy snort of a horse not too far away. His eyes strained into the darkness but he was unable to detect any sign of life or flames from a fire, but his unerring sense of direction had pin-pointed the sound and was reinforced when he heard it again.

"Bout 300 yards up an' a few yards off the trail, I'd say,' he said to himself.

'You gonna take a look-see who they is?' he replied.

'Sure am!' he confirmed. 'I like to know who is where an' how many of 'em there are.'

'You is quite mad! You know that don't you?'

'It'd be even madder if we didn't know who they was!'

'This whole thing is mad! OK, let's go an' get it over an' done with. At least we'll know who killed us!'

He crept forward, this time taking to the line of trees on the opposite side of the trail to where he knew them to be camped. Of necessity, his progress was very slow, feeling his way forward very gingerly, stopping several times to avoid or move dead branches. He did not know how good the three men were at detecting the sound of a branch being broken underfoot, but he was pretty certain that the Indians would be able to detect such things.

Eventually he crouched in the cover of a large bush and peered across the trail. Camped about twenty yards away, he could see at least three figures highlighted against the glow of a fire and, although they were not talking too loudly, he could hear the murmur of voices.

They appeared to be camped in the lee of a large rock. From the snatches of conversation that he could hear, he assumed that they were the three men who used to work for Mitchell, but he had to be quite sure. He crossed the trail and made his way behind the large rock, hoping that he would be able to scale it and look down on them. In the event it proved impossible, at least in-so-far as he would not be able to scale it without giving himself away.

He very slowly edged himself round to the far side of it and it proved to be rather larger than he had imagined. However, he was soon able to peer round the edge of it and look down onto the camp, now some ten feet below and to his right. His assumption had proved correct; they were the three men from Abbotsville, he easily recognized one of them. Their horses were tethered about ten yards away and seemed a little uneasy. He had to assume that it was his presence which spooked them, so he withdrew behind the rock.

'You could take 'em out easy enough,' he said to himself.

'Probably,' he agreed, 'but we don't know where them Indians is. Any shootin' now is sure to bring 'em runnin', an' I could do without any more problems. If they find 'em dead, they'll know someone else is around, even if they don't know already.'

'If they don't know 'bout us, you can bet your boots they know 'bout them,' he said.

'I'm countin' on it! OK, let's go see if we can see the Indians, an' then we'll get back an' get some shut-eye.'

'Forget the Indians!' he advised himself. 'If they is about I reckon we'll come across 'em soon enough.'

'Maybe you is right, but I'd still like to take a look-see.'

'You're mad!'

'I know! Makes life interestin' though, don't it?'

He made his way back to the trail and followed it for about another half hour, stopping at various vantage points to scan the terrain ahead, but he was unable to detect anything. At the last vantage point, a large, high and flat rock, he was just about to turn back when he detected the slightest trace of flickering light.

'A fire!' he whispered. 'It's gotta be them.'

'OK, so now you've found 'em, let's get back.'

'Could be someone else,' he reasoned. 'Other folk do travel.'

'That's their business, not ours,' he said.

'We gotta be sure,' he insisted. 'We is goin' to find out.'

'They is Indians, remember,' he said. 'We might not be able to get that close to 'em without being detected.'

'Chance we gotta take,' he said.

His eyes strained the darkness again for confirmation of the exact location of the light. It was very faint, but he managed to pick it out and started off along the trail towards it. About 200 yards further on, the trail veered around to the right and, although he had travelled that way before, he had not been taking too much notice of its twists and turns, so he did not know if it veered back to the left or not. He decided that he had better not trust to fortune and went up among the trees to his left.

He was pretty certain that he was heading in the right direction and his instinct was proved correct as he came out of the trees on to a flat area which, he could just make out, seemed to disappear in a sharp drop. After checking to see if there were any lookouts posted, which there did not seem to be, he made his way forward.

He suddenly dropped flat on the ground as he neared what he thought was a steep drop, finding that it was not as deep or as sheer as he had expected. From where he was he could see the fire quite easily and around it were dotted the sleeping forms of perhaps eight or ten men. There was one lone man huddled by the fire but it was impossible to tell if they were Indians or half-breeds. He waited for quite some time before the man by the fire moved.

He was dressed in the kind of clothing most men wore but, like quite a lot of Indian tribes, his hair, caught briefly by the light of the fire, was shoulder length and tied at the back. Brogan did not know of many white men who wore their hair in this fashion and, under the circumstances, he had to assume that these men were in fact the Indian bandits Pete had told him about.

Having satisfied his curiosity, he eased himself backwards and disappeared amongst the trees to make his way back to Pete. The journey took longer than he had expected. He knew he had not travelled very fast, but it seemed that he had covered more ground than he had imagined.

Finding his way back to Pete was easy enough; as ever, he had made mental notes of landmarks and certain trees to guide him. He was very surprised to find Pete still sitting by his saddle.

'Bang! You is dead!' he whispered in Pete's ear.

'I heard you!' said Pete.

'How'd you know it was me?'

'Who else could it be?' Pete asked simply.

'Could've been a mountain lion,' said Brogan.

'Not in these parts,' said Pete. 'There ain't been no mountain lions around here for years. They was all killed off by the settlers 'cos they was a threat to their animals.'

'OK, so it warn't a mountain lion. Could've been one of them though.'

'At this time of night? Only mad men like you go out there at night.'

'Worth it though,' said Brogan, settling down by his saddle.

'You found 'em?' Pete seemed very interested.

'I found 'em,' confirmed Brogan. 'Both lots.'

'Close?'

'Close enough, I'll tell you about it in the mornin'. Now, you drunk all that whisky?'

'Thought you didn't like whisky?'

'I don't that much,' said Brogan. 'But it's cold out there an' since I said no fire, I guess I'll have a swig just to warm me up a bit.'

Pete laughed slightly and handed Brogan a bottle. 'Drink it all,' he invited. 'I've had my fill.'

'Thanks,' said Brogan, uncorking the bottle and raising it to his lips. There was not that much left, but it was enough to send a surge of warmth through Brogan's body. When he had finished it, he drew his blanket across him and went to sleep. He had expected Pete to be more inquisitive, but either Pete was not or the whisky had taken away his ability to ask.

FIVE

'BASTARD!' screamed Pete as he frantically searched around. 'Bastard! He's done a runner with the money! Never should have trusted him ... ' His tirade was cut short by a snort from behind a large bush. 'Where are you, McNally? Come on out!' He drew his ancient Adams and ran behind the bush to find Brogan's horse and he stood there rather bewildered. 'What the hell's goin' on? He can't've run out.' He went back to where they had slept and found Brogan's saddle still there.

'No, I didn't run out!' a voice said from behind him.

'Brogan! What the hell you playin' at? The money's gone. What you done with it?'

'Just a little insurance,' said Brogan, coming into view, smiling.

'Insurance? What you talkin' about? Where's the money?'

'Safe enough,' said Brogan. 'We'll collect it later. Right now we'd better be on our way. I'll explain as we go.'

Pete sighed. 'It'd better be good. If we don't get it back Mr Mitchell is gonna be mighty sore.'

'It's OK I tell you,' said Brogan. 'Now get saddled up an' let's go while we can.'

Pete sighed again but did not ask any more questions and saddled his mule while Brogan saddled his horse. They were soon on their way, at first following the trail, but after a couple of miles, Brogan led the way off the trail and through the trees.

'What we goin' this way for?' demanded Pete. 'An' maybe now you'll tell me what the hell's goin' on.'

'We is goin' this way to avoid them three men from Abbotsville,' said Brogan. 'As for the money, I got to thinkin' last night after we'd bedded down. Them Indians an' half-breeds is camped up ahead an' if what you say is right, they won't try an' kill us.'

'I don't reckon they will. Ain't much point in that, they know they'll be hunted outa these hills if they do.'

'That's what I figured,' said Brogan. 'So, early this mornin' I took the satchel an' went on ahead an' hid it well past where they is camped. When we is past 'em, we collect it an' get on our way.'

'An' just what was the point of hidin' it?' demanded Pete.

'Simple!' Brogan grinned. 'We let 'em see us but when they do, they'll find we ain't got no money.'

'An' you reckon that is gonna fool 'em?' Pete sneered. 'Well I don't. They'll soon realize they've been had an' come after us.'

'Nothin' more certain,' Brogan agreed, 'but it gives us a head start. We'll worry about 'em later.'

'Don't see how it's gonna help. They'll smell a rat from the start. They know I wouldn't be makin' the journey without the money.'

'If we meet 'em, you just agree with everythin' I say. Got that? No matter what I say, you just agree with it.'

'OK, I'll go along with it. I must be thick, I can't see how it's gonna help us at all.'

Brogan just laughed lightly and indicated that they continue their detour in silence. After about half an hour they turned back on to the main trail again and followed it for about another twenty minutes before Brogan warned Pete that they were almost on top of the bandits. Almost as he said it, he indicated the trees either side.

'We got company!' he announced.

'Hold it right there!' came a command.

'We're holdin' it!' Brogan called. 'What you want?'

Five men, one white, two obviously full blooded Indians and two he assumed to be half-breeds came out of the cover of the trees, rifles at the ready. Brogan made no attempt to go for his gun.

The man who appeared to be the leader of the group, a full blooded Indian, sneered and came forward. 'The old man knows what we want,' he said. 'He knows the routine.'

'If it's the payroll you want,' said Brogan, 'we ain't got it.'

'Bullshit!' sneered the Indian. 'Hand it over an' you won't get hurt. Pete knows we never hurt him.'

'Sure, we had the payroll,' said Brogan. 'We had it up to about an hour ago, but we ain't got it now. Ain't that right, Pete?' Pete nodded. 'Search us if you want, you won't find it.'

The Indian looked very puzzled. 'Search!' he commanded one of the others. The man made a thorough search and eventually shook his head. 'So you do not have it! Where is it?'

'You got some competition,' said Brogan. 'Three men Mitchell fired a couple of days ago.'

'We know them!' the Indian said, still not believing Brogan.

'Then I reckon you also know they tried to rob Pete. That's why they was fired.'

'Are you telling me that these men have stolen the payroll?'

'That's exactly what I am tellin' you,' confirmed Brogan. 'I said we had the payroll up till about an hour ago. We was waylaid by 'em an' they took the money.'

'Is this so?' the Indian demanded of Pete.

'Sure is,' replied Pete, glancing briefly at Brogan. 'Brogan here was sent with me to try an' make sure I got through. We was expectin' some sort of trouble from you, but we never figured on them. We thought they'd ridden outa the territory. That's why they was able to take us so easy. They was suddenly there, we didn't have no chance.'

'It makes sense,' said the lone white man, a young man barely out of his teens. 'I remember sayin' I couldn't understand why they was hangin' about.'

'I remember,' the Indian said. 'Yes, I can see now. However, it does not make sense that you go on to the mines. Why do you do so?'

'Mr Mitchell's instructions,' said Brogan. 'The payroll should've been there a couple of days ago. He said that if we was robbed, we was to ride on an' tell the foreman what had happened, so's he could tell the miners. Mitchell was worried they'd all down tools if they didn't get their money. Ain't that right, Pete?'

'His exact words,' confirmed Pete.

'And where are these men now?' asked the Indian.

'That's anybody's guess,' said Brogan. 'They didn't come this way, that's for sure.'

'We know where they are camped,' said the Indian. 'They cannot escape us no matter where they go.' He nodded at the others. 'We go, we get back the money that is ours. Jim, you go tell the others, we will wait here.' Jim, the white man, nodded and disappeared among the trees.

'Can we get on our way?' asked Brogan. 'Them miners is sure to be gettin' mighty restless.'

'You may go!' said the Indian. 'And you can tell Mitchell that he will have no more trouble from them.'

'Thanks,' said Brogan. 'Remember though, they is all pretty useful with guns.'

'Not like some old man, you mean!' The Indian laughed. 'I would not worry about us, we can look after ourselves.'

'Can't say as I was worryin' about you,' said Brogan. 'Just thought I'd better warn you. I don't care who kills who.'

'Nor do I!' The Indian raised his rifle at Brogan. 'I could kill you both now and probably nobody would ever find your bodies. They would think that it was you who ran off with the money.'

'You could,' said Brogan calmly, 'but it wouldn't do you no good. I reckon that's why you never killed Pete. As soon as you did that, there'd be more armed men up here than you could cope with. As for them thinkin' I'd run off with the money, Sheriff Dempster wouldn't buy it. I had the opportunity before but I didn't take it.'

'You are probably right,' agreed the Indian, lowering the rifle. 'Now go while you can.'

'C'mon, Pete,' said Brogan. 'We've got a long ride ahead.'

Pete urged his mule into an unaccustomed trot and followed Brogan. They travelled for about another two miles before Brogan called a halt.

'You flew pretty close to the wind back there,' puffed Pete. 'I thought he was goin' to kill us.'

'I didn't,' said Brogan. 'I can usually tell by the look in a feller's eyes if he has that in mind. He was just lettin' us know who was the boss.'

'If you say so,' said Pete. 'So where's the money then?'

'Over there!' He nodded at a large tree. 'I buried

it in the roots.' He leapt off his horse and clawed
at the earth, eventually raising the satchel. 'Still
intact!' he announced. 'C'mon, let's get goin'. See if
you can get that mule of yours to go a bit faster,
we is gonna need all the start we can get.'

'She ain't used to runnin',' said Pete. 'I'll try
though.'

'Jab her arse or somethin',' suggested Brogan.

'That'll only make her more stubborn,' said
Pete. 'I've tried that a few times.'

'Then just make her go as fast as you can!'

'They are still in camp!' one of the half-breeds
announced. 'They seem very sure of themselves.'

'Spread out, surround them!' ordered the
leader. 'Do not be afraid to shoot, nobody is going
to worry too much about them.'

The ten men spread out, five going to one side
and five to the other with a swiftness and
quietness that even Brogan would have found
difficult to detect. When he thought that his men
had had enough time to get themselves into
position, the leader suddenly showed himself, his
rifle at the ready.

'Do not try to go for your guns!' he rasped. 'You
are completely surrounded.'

'What the hell do you want?' demanded the
leader of the three men. 'We ain't got nothin'
worth takin'.'

'You have a lot worth taking,' said the Indian.
'You have money you have stolen from the old
man and the one who looks like a saddle tramp.'

'Money!' exclaimed the man. 'Oh yeh, I see. Sure, we took the money off that old man, but that was three days ago an' we never got away with it. Saddle tramp? Tall, lean guy, smells like a midden?'

'It could be the same man. Do not lie to us, it will do you no good. If you want to remain alive, hand over the money.'

'We ain't got the money, I tell you! That saddle-bum came along an' took us by surprise. He took us into Abbotsville, but Mitchell let us go.'

'You are lying!' He nodded to the others. 'Search!'

A thorough search of the area proved fruitless and the Indian leader's patience was beginning to grow thin.

'What have you done with the money?' he demanded. 'We know that you have it.'

'You searched an' you didn't find it,' said the man. 'I've already told you, we did take it off the old man, but that was three days ago.'

'You lie!' snapped the Indian. 'We know that you stole it this morning, the old man and the saddle tramp told us so.'

'Then they know more than we do,' said one of the others. 'We ain't seen hide nor hair of either of 'em.'

'Then why do you stay here?' the Indian demanded again.

''Cos we did intend to take the payroll,' the leader of the three admitted. 'Sure, we admit it, but we ain't seen either of 'em since we rode outa Abbotsville.'

'If they told you we'd taken the money, they is lyin'!' said one of the others. 'An' if that saddlebum had been with the old man, he'd've been dead by now.'

'The money sure ain't here,' said Jim, the young white man. 'I dunno, but I had me this feelin' that that saddlebum was spinnin' us a yarn.'

'But they did not have it either,' the Indian pointed out.

'Then maybe there never was any money,' Jim suggested.

'They would not be making the journey without it! Besides, did they not say that they had it but these three had taken it from them. If they never had it, why should they say they had? They must have known they were here, otherwise they would not have made up such a story.'

'I can't argue with that,' agreed Jim. 'I don't know how they did it, but they sure pulled the wool over our eyes.'

'It will do them no good!' The Indian sneered. 'They travel on an old mule and a worn out old horse, they cannot get far.'

'What about them?' Jim asked, nodding at the three men.

'Trash!' The Indian spat on the ground. 'We should kill them.'

'What you wanna kill us for?' quavered one of the men. 'We ain't done no harm to you.'

'You come to steal that which is ours!' The Indian spat again. 'This is our land, only we can steal from anyone who travels this way. Have you not said that it was your intention to steal from the old man?'

'Yeh, it was,' said the leader of the three. 'I guess we was wrong though. We'll just pack up an' get the hell out of it.'

'For your own sakes, you had better do so,' said the Indian. 'The only thing that saves your lives is that if it is discovered that we have killed you, it will bring the army who will force our people to hand us over to them. Be on your way while it is still in my mind to let you go. But beware, if it is that you have taken the money and have hidden it somewhere, you will be followed and watched until you are away from this place.'

'I can assure you we ain't got the money, nor have we set eyes on the old man or the saddlebum. Like your friend says, it looks like they put one over on you somehow. I hope you catch 'em an' you can do us a favour.'

'A favour! What favour can you ask of us?'

'Kill the saddlebum. Real slow an' painful like I hear you Indians can do.'

'If you are not away from here in two minutes, it is you who will suffer the slow death!'

'We're goin'!' the leader assured. 'Right now.'

Since their horses were already saddled, the three lost no time in mounting up and riding out back along the trail that led to Abbotsville. The Indian leader despatched two men to follow them and ordered another search of the area, which still yielded nothing and eventually he called his men together and told them they were going after

Brogan and Pete.

'Do not kill either of them unless you have to,' he ordered. 'I do not know what they have done or how they have done it, but I want them both alive!'

Brogan and Pete had made good headway, but Brogan knew that it was only a matter of time before their ruse would be discovered and the bandits would be hot on their trail.

'You say there's other ways through?' Brogan asked Pete.

'Sure. It'll take a little longer, but it can be done.'

'Then you'd better find one,' said Brogan. 'By my reckoning them Indians have just found they've been had an' they'll be mighty sore about it. The quicker we is off this trail the better.'

'They is used to trackin', remember,' said Pete.

'And I'm used to coverin' my tracks,' said Brogan.

'There's a way not too far ahead,' said Pete. 'I hope you got as good a head for heights as I have, you is gonna need it.'

'Just show me the way,' said Brogan.

''Bout half a mile off to the left,' said Pete. 'It ain't too bad for the first mile or so, but then you gotta follow a deer track along the top of a ravine.'

'If the deer can do it, so can we,' said Brogan.

They turned off the main trail where Pete indicated and almost immediately Brogan dismounted and began to obliterate their tracks, to which Pete announced that he did not think it was going to fool them for long.

'Maybe not,' said Brogan. 'I wasn't countin' on it,

but it'll buy us a bit more time.' He remounted and nodded to Pete to lead on since he knew the way.

Brogan had cut a small sapling which he dragged behind them in an attempt to hide signs of their progress. Even he knew that an experienced tracker would quickly see what had happened, but he felt he had to try something.

'Maybe this idea warn't such a good one after all,' he said to Pete as they approached the ravine. 'All them Indians've gotta do is sit an' wait for us where we join the main trail again. I reckon they must know where it comes out.'

'Sure, they most likely know,' agreed Pete. 'Sittin' waitin' for us on the trail won't do 'em no good though. Once we're past the ravine there's three ways to go. Two lead back to the trail an' the third cuts across the top of the hills almost to where the mines are. I reckon they've got two choices. They can follow us or try an' cut us off by ridin' along the trail an' then doublin' back, but that's a long way round.'

'Or they could do both,' Brogan pointed out. 'There's enough of 'em to do that. They'd have us nicely bottled up.'

'Could do, I suppose,' said Pete. 'Never thought of that.' He laughed quietly. 'I'd sure like to've seen their faces when they found out they'd been had.'

'They won't fall for it a second time, that's for sure,' said Brogan. 'I guess I'll have to think of somethin' else next time, if there is a next time.'

'You can count on it!' Pete grinned. 'Even if we

get through, we gotta go back, remember that. They won't be too kindly disposed to just lettin' us ride on through. They'll be pretty mad at you, they'll know it was your idea. Maybe they won't kill you, but they can sure make life uncomfortable for a while.'

'I reckon I can cope with anythin' they throw at me,' said Brogan. 'If I can't, I've only got myself to blame.'

They were now following a narrow deer track along the edge of the ravine, the bottom of which was about a hundred feet below and very rocky. Water rushed along the bottom, bouncing and twisting over the rocks. The trail was, at some points, quite literally the edge of the ravine, forced that way by large boulders or rocky outcrops. It was quite impossible to travel further away from the ravine as that side was nothing but a few feet of loose scree backing onto sheer cliffs of about fifty feet.

'How far does this go on?' asked Brogan.

'I dunno for sure,' Pete admitted. 'Maybe fifteen miles. I ain't never been to the end of it, never had the need. About twelve miles on it turns pretty sharp to the left, that's where we leave it an' go straight on.'

'Twelve miles!' Brogan sighed. 'I reckon that's gonna take us most the day at this rate.'

'Yeh, an' we're lucky. I had to come this way once when it was rainin' an' it took the best part of two days. This track is worse'n slippery elm when it's wet.'

'I can believe it too,' said Brogan. 'Still, if it's hard for us, it's gonna be just as hard for them.'

'Wouldn't count on it,' said Pete, with a smile. 'It could be they know some other ways I don't.'

'That's the kind of comfort I could do without!' Brogan laughed.

At about midday, they stopped at one of the very few flat areas to rest their animals and have a bite to eat. This time Brogan had no objection to the lighting of a fire. They finished off the dry bread and cheese Pete had brought along and Brogan was really appreciative of some hot coffee. When they had eaten, Brogan ascended the scree and clambered up the cliff which, at that point was no more than twenty feet high.

At the top, he looked over a large plateau, the flatness broken here and there by a few trees or bushes. It may have looked flat, but he knew from experience that it was pitted with ravines just like the one they had travelled along. However, it had not been his intention to admire the scenery; his purpose had been to look along the ravine for signs of life – signs that they were either being followed or that there was someone ahead trying to cut them off. His keen eyes studied the land, noting every movement of bird and animal, looking for movements that did not belong.

Whether he saw something, he could not be certain, but his senses told him that there were others following. Working on the assumption that half of them would follow and half would try to head them off, he surveyed the immediate area of the ravine for possible alternative ways through.

About half a mile ahead, the track seemed to dip almost down to the bottom of the ravine, sent that way by what appeared to be a land slip blocking the way across the top. He returned to Pete and asked him about it.

'Happened about four years ago,' said Pete. 'It's easy enough though, even if it is a bit steep.'

'Is there a way across?'

'Only if you is a fish,' said Pete. 'An' even if you do reach the other side, there ain't no way up.'

'Ever been on the other side?'

'No, never had no cause,' said Pete.

'Well I reckon we got cause now,' said Brogan. 'I'm certain we're bein' followed an' I gotta assume there's more of 'em up ahead. So, it seems logical to me to cross over.'

'Can't argue with that,' Pete said. 'Only trouble is, there ain't no way across, not unless you can fly.'

Brogan sighed. 'Yeh, I kinda figured that. Still, even if we can't cross, them followin' us can't do nothin'. They must know they'd never get close enough. We could pick 'em off easy enough.'

'I reckon they know it,' agreed Pete. 'They've still got the advantage though an' that's time. They got all the time in the world, we ain't.'

'We've got as much time as they've got,' said Brogan. 'That don't help us much though. OK, let's go, we'll have to take our chance with 'em I suppose.'

Brogan studied the narrow ravine from where

the track had been forced downwards and had to agree with Pete's idea that even if they could get across, there was no way they were going to scale the sheer walls on the other side.

They slowly edged their way down the track, now largely made up of scree and more than once both horse and mule threatened to plunge off the edge into the swirling water. Once they were safely at the bottom they rested, but Brogan was uneasy. He felt very insecure down there; anyone could have quite easily picked them off from above. He was all for moving on when a solitary deer suddenly bolted up the track.

'Where in the hell did he come from?' Brogan said, almost to himself. 'I never saw him.'

'You oughta know you can ride right past a deer an' not see it,' said Pete. 'We probably passed a few on the way up here.'

'Two,' said Brogan. 'I saw 'em. I sure didn't see that one till he spooked himself though.'

'It seems to bother you,' said Pete.

'Sure it does,' said Brogan. 'I don't miss things like that. Where'd he come from?'

'Darned if I know,' said Pete. 'Don't see what's botherin' you either. It's only a deer.'

'Yeh,' agreed Brogan. 'It's only a deer!'

Instead of accepting the fact, Brogan began to search around where the deer had started from, much to Pete's amusement and even slight annoyance. Suddenly he gave a whoop of delight and bounded back across the rocks to Pete.

'What in tarnation's gotten into you?' exclaimed

Pete. 'You look like you just found the mother-lode.'

'Maybe I have!' Brogan laughed. 'It'll sure give 'em somethin' to think about.'

'There you go again!' objected Pete. 'Talkin' in riddles.'

'Come take a look,' urged Brogan, leading the way back across the rocks to the far side of the pool that had been formed by the collapse of the face. Pete sighed, complained that he was not as young as he used to be, but followed Brogan across, hardly bothering with the rocks as stepping stones, simply splashing through the water. He joined Brogan and peered behind a large boulder.

'So what?' he muttered. 'You dragged me all the way over here just to look at some hole in the rock! If we don't get outa here, we'll be trapped.'

'Are you blind, or thick or somethin'?' demanded Brogan. 'Just you take another look!'

Pete obliged and took another cursory look. 'Still looks like a hole in the rock to me!'

'That's exactly what it is!' exclaimed Brogan.

'I reckon it's you what's thick, not me,' said Pete. 'So you found a hole in the rock! I don't see what you're gettin' so hell-fire excited about. That's all it is, a hole in the rock!'

SIX

Brogan shook his head and sighed. 'You is missin' the point. We've got bandits front an' back of us, we need somewhere to hide. This hole'll take our animals easy enough.'

'Yeh, I reckon it will!' said Pete, slowly turning to look at Brogan. 'Hell, Brogan!' he croaked. 'That ain't half a bad idea. I never knew this hole was here an' I reckon I know this territory as well as any man.'

'An' the chances are they probably don't either,' said Brogan. He peered over into the hole. 'Deer can get in an' out easy enough, they can climb an' jump but I'd like to see my old horse get her arse in there.'

'An' I'm darned sure Esmerelda wouldn't even try,' said Pete. 'Looks like we gotta shift a few rocks.'

'Only trouble with that is anyone with half an eye would see they'd been moved. I'm goin' inside to see what gives.'

He eased himself into the hole easily enough and went inside a couple of yards, where he found himself in a fairly large chamber, roughly fifteen feet across by about ten feet high. There did not appear to be any other ways in or out nor passages off. However, the glint of sunlight in the water which extended into the cave a few feet made him crouch and look.

He checked that the light was not a reflection from the entrance behind him and then stood up, braced himself against the wall and slowly felt all round, down to water level. At about eighteen inches above the water, although he could not see it, there was an arch which appeared to lead out into the pool behind. He dropped to his knees and gingerly lowered his arm into the icy water and felt down into the depths as far as he could, almost falling in in the process. He sat back on his haunches and sighed.

'Only one way to find out just how deep it is, get in there an' see if you can get through.' He laughed quietly. 'My ma allus said I should learn to swim!' He called back to Pete. 'Can you swim?' There was a scuffling and Pete puffed alongside him.

'Swim! What the hell for?' Brogan pointed at the water. 'Sure, I can swim. I thought everybody could swim.'

'I can't,' admitted Brogan. 'Swimmin's too close to bathin', it ain't healthy.'

'More healthy than drownin'!' laughed Pete. 'See what you're gettin' at though. How deep is it?'

'That's why I asked if you could swim,' said Brogan. 'I can't touch the bottom with my arm in the water.'

'An' you want me to go in there an' see if we can get your horse an' my mule through that way? It could mean 'em havin' to go under water.'

'I don't reckon so,' said Brogan. 'If you feel about eighteen inches above, there's an arch an' I reckon it goes straight through.'

'I only hope this works,' said Pete. 'I'd hate to get wet for nothin'!' He did not wait for Brogan to say anything else, nor to take any of his clothes off. Suddenly he slid into the water, gave a brief cry as the coldness hit him and, with a great splash, submerged himself.

Brogan watched anxiously and for a few seconds Pete remained submerged but his head appeared briefly, Brogan guessed under the arch, and then disappeared again. Coughing and spluttering from outside made Brogan smile and he went to look over the large rock across the entrance.

'Christ! It's bloody cold!' Pete wheezed.

'How deep?' asked Brogan.

''Bout ten feet at the most.' Pete shuddered as he came out of the water. 'Seems to slope up inside. It should be easy enough to get 'em through that way, providin' we can even get 'em into the water in the first place.'

'We'll get 'em in!' Brogan laughed. 'Get them packs an' saddles off 'em first though.'

They unsaddled both animals and Brogan offered to let his horse go first. She was obviously not very keen on the idea and had to be pulled by Pete and pushed by Brogan. Brogan went back into the cave and waited for Pete to appear and when he did, he took hold of the reins and pulled with all his might. Eventually his horse clambered out of the water inside the cave, protesting loudly. The operation was repeated with Pete's mule and, rather surprisingly, she proved quite co-operative.

'One more job to do,' said Pete. 'Since I'm soaked through, I might as well make it look like we climbed up the track. I'll jump back into the pool from the top. It should be OK.'

Brogan did not try to stop him. He realized that it was a very good idea and rather regretted that he could not swim. He watched Pete clamber up the track, leaving very obvious signs and, almost at the top, Pete stood for a moment on the edge, looking nervously down into the pool now some twenty-five feet below him. Suddenly he launched himself into the air. The noise of the splash was largely drowned by the general noise of rushing water about them, and Pete seemed to remain submerged for quite a long time, but his head suddenly appeared and he swam to the submerged entrance. Coughing and spluttering, he entered the cave and flopped in an untidy heap on the floor.

'Don't suppose we can have a fire?' he asked, shuddering with cold. 'I'm bloody frozen!'

'You got some dry clothes?' asked Brogan.

'Underwear an' a shirt, that's all,' replied Pete.

'Then get stripped off an' put 'em on,' advised Brogan. 'I ain't got me no spares.'

'No fire?' repeated Pete.

'Not yet,' said Brogan. 'We got no way of tellin' where the smoke'll go. C'mon, get outa them wet things, at least we should be able to dry 'em out a bit.'

Pete was soon out of his wet clothes and in his dry ones. Brogan, in the meantime, had been crouched at the entrance looking and listening.

'We got company!' he whispered. 'Have your rifle ready, just in case we need to shoot.'

'If this don't work, we is sittin' ducks in here,' said Pete, checking his rifle.

Brogan positioned himself where he could see the track down to the pool and about ten minutes later, three men, probably half-breeds, appeared at the top and looked down. Words passed between them, which Brogan could not make out, and very slowly they made their way down the steep track on foot and leading their horses. Brogan prayed that neither man nor horse would lose their footing. Any accident could only serve to help anyone find them. He breathed a sigh of relief as the three men reached the pool in safety. They all scooped mouthfuls of water and allowed their horses to drink their fill.

'This way, and not too long ago!' said one of the half-breeds, pointing to the track away from the pool.

'Let them go,' said one of the others. 'We must not get too close, not just yet. We stay here for another ten minutes.'

Brogan silently cursed and gripped his rifle a

little tighter. It would have been a relatively simple matter to shoot all three but there were two reasons why he chose not to. Firstly, there was no way of telling exactly where the rest of them were and secondly, he had an aversion to killing anyone if his life was not in immediate danger and he felt that even if they had known where they were hiding, they would not have attempted to kill either of them.

However, his grip on his rifle became even tighter when one of them suddenly stared, apparently straight at him, for some time and then waded into the pool as if making for the entrance. He stopped and bent down to pick something out of the water, which he held up for the others to see.

'One of them dropped this!' he called, holding up what looked like a piece of rag.

'So what?' came the reply. 'You can keep it if you want it.'

The man grunted and threw the rag back into the water and returned to his companions. A few minutes later they clambered up the track, their own slippings and slidings obliterating all the signs made by Pete, which Brogan decided was a good thing.

'OK, so what we do now?' asked Pete, after the half-breeds had gone. 'Double back or somethin'?

'We sit tight,' said Brogan. 'We got no idea where they'll meet up with the others, but when they do, they is gonna start searchin'. They missed us once, maybe they'll miss us again.'

'Fat chance of that!' Pete scowled. 'I say we get the hell outa here now.'

'An' go where?'

'Anywhere away from here,' said Pete. 'I'd feel safer out in open country than cooped up like a chicken.'

'I gotta confess, so would I!' admitted Brogan.

The two groups stared at each other, obviously very bewildered. They had met up at the point where the ravine swung sharp left and three distinct trails fanned out. Two of them led back to the main trail and the other eventually came out by the mines.

'You must have ridden straight past them!' complained the Indian leader. 'They have not come this way.'

'It is you who must have been asleep and they walked past you!' retorted the leader of the three half-breeds. 'The track along the ravine is too narrow, it is impossible for anyone to hide, you know that as well as I do!'

'How far in front of you were they?' demanded the leader.

'Perhaps twenty minutes, half an hour at the most!'

'And we have been here for more than an hour! It is impossible, they must be back there somewhere!'

'I think not!' replied the half-breed. 'But you will have your way. Come let us return and you will see.'

Brogan had reluctantly agreed with Pete that they had had to get out of the cave as soon as possible, but he was against the idea of following the deer track again, in any direction. It was Pete who had suggested that since they were down in the water they should try and follow the swirling river until they could climb up the opposite side. Brogan had looked with a great deal of misgiving at the torrent, thought about not being able to swim but swallowed his misgivings and agreed.

Getting horse and mule out of the cave proved more difficult than getting them in but, after about fifteen minutes, they were all outside and soaking wet. Pete complained that he had no more dry clothes and cursed Brogan for not being able to swim.

There was a fairly steep drop from the pool down into another large pool but both horse and mule negotiated the slippery stones with remarkable ease. Once in the lower pool, Brogan had a problem; it was too deep for him to stand or walk and the sides were completely sheer for about twenty feet or more on both sides. The only thing he could do was cling to his horse.

The fifty yards of the pool were negotiated with ease but the next sixty or seventy yards were more difficult; even though the water was shallow, it cascaded and swirled with almost terrifying force at some points, threatening to sweep both men and animals away. After a few tense moments, they had overcome the worst of it. Suddenly, Pete pointed ahead.

'I reckon we can get up there!' he cried.

Another rock fall had created a very rocky slope almost to the top of the ravine and Brogan had to agree that it seemed to offer them their only chance. They stood at the bottom and examined it.

'Yeh, I reckon we can get 'em up there! Best thing would be if I was to go up top first an' you was to tie the rope around their necks an' I'll try an' pull 'em up.'

Brogan made the top very easily and threw the rope down. Pete secured his mule first and, at Brogan's signal, gave her a prod with a sharp stick. The mule bellowed briefly, started to pull against the rope, but eventually decided that it was easier to go upwards. She climbed up almost unaided. Brogan's horse was not as sure footed as the mule, but eventually she too was at the top. It was just after Pete had puffed and wheezed his way up that Brogan suddenly pulled horse and mule into the cover of some thick bushes and silently urged Pete to follow.

Brogan counted them as they rode past on the other side. Ten of them, all young men in their late teens or early twenties and probably full of wild ideas. Whilst Brogan had found that such young men lacked experience and expertise, they were often more dangerous than other outlaws because they were so unpredictable.

'You say you've never been this side of the ravine before?' said Brogan, after the troupe had passed. Pete shook his head. 'Then it's somethin' new for both of us. Come on, let's get goin'.'

'We'll catch our death of pneumonia or somethin'!' Pete complained.

'Very probably!' agreed Brogan. 'Which is one reason I don't believe in bathin', it ain't natural. Still, it did get us away from them.'

'I reckon it would've been easier to've just given 'em the money! They'll like as not get it anyhow.'

'Maybe they will, maybe they won't,' said Brogan. 'How much further is it to the mines?'

'On the other side, maybe twenty miles,' said Pete. 'Almost certainly more on this an' I reckon we gotta cross the ravine again somehow.'

'Twenty miles!' Brogan looked up at the sky. 'About two hours to sundown I reckon. C'mon, let's find somewhere to hole up.'

'Somewheres where we can have a fire!' said Pete, with a growl.

'Sure thing,' agreed Brogan.

It was easier riding on that side of the ravine, although it was still not possible to get too far away from the edge. They passed the point where the ravine took a sharp left turn and continued for another hour before Brogan pulled up at a point well back from the ravine under the cover of an overhanging rock. He immediately set to gathering brush and kindling wood for the fire.

What food they had had been ruined by the water but that did not bother Brogan too much; he was used to living off the land and in a matter of minutes had caught a large lizard and located various edible bulbs resembling onions.

'I heard 'bout folk like you,' said Pete, eyeing the lizard doubtfully. 'I even heard you ain't above eatin' bugs an' things.'

'I ain't never had to come down to eatin' bugs,' said Brogan. 'I met some Indians what do though, mainly 'cos they got hardly anythin' else. You never tasted lizard before? It ain't exactly my favourite food, but it ain't half bad, 'specially when you ain't eaten for a few days.'

'I reckon I can go without food for a while,' said Pete.

'All the more for me!' Brogan laughed.

Pete began to have second thoughts about not eating when the vegetables started to boil in Brogan's pot and the lizard sizzled as it roasted in front of the fire.

'Guess I am kinda hungry,' said Pete, licking his lips. 'I ain't never been one for not tryin' anythin' new.'

Brogan laughed and ladled out a helping and handed him a portion of lizard. Pete looked at it dubiously but forced himself to taste it.

'Good?' asked Brogan.

'Ain't half bad!' admitted Pete. 'Kinda like veal or deer meat.' He sniffed at the vegetables and tasted them. 'Onions! Not your regular onions though, these taste stronger, but they is better'n nothin'. Where'd you learn to tell what is good to eat? I hear tell that if you ain't careful, some of these things is poisonous.'

'Experience!' said Brogan. 'Experience an' I

done me a bit of learnin' off the Indians. It ain't
often that there ain't nothin' at all to eat, even out
in the desert. There's usually somethin' there if'n
you know where to look.'

'Even water?'

'Even water,' confirmed Brogan. 'Or at least
somethin' that does the same job, usually cactus.'

'Yeh, I tried cactus once,' said Pete. 'Almost
made me sick. Tasted foul it did.'

'It sure tastes sweet when you ain't had proper
water for a few days though.'

They finished their meal in silence, Pete even
finishing off the lizard and Brogan stretched out
some of his wet clothes around the fire and
huddled near the flames in his underclothes. Pete
decided to do the same.

'So what's your plan now?' asked Pete.

'I ain't got no plan,' said Brogan. 'I don't see
much point in makin' plans, 'specially when I
know nothin' about where I am or where I'm goin'.
We'll carry on along the ravine until we can find
somewhere to cross an' then trust to luck we make
it to the mines.'

'Just supposin', for argument's sake,' said Pete,
'that we do make it to the mines. What you gonna
do then? You've gotta get back to Abbotsville to
collect your money. I don't reckon them Indians
an' half-breeds is gonna be too kindly disposed.
You've gotta get past them, remember.'

'Maybe I'll just forget about the money,' said
Brogan.

'That'd be kinda stupid, especially after riskin''

your life gettin' out.'

'Maybe so!' Brogan shrugged. 'Like I say, I'll worry 'bout that later. Right now I'm gonna get me some shut-eye.'

SEVEN

They were on their way just as dawn broke and, as the sun was just climbing above the surrounding hills about two hours later, the ravine suddenly gave way to easier ground. It was not flat, but not so steep nor so thickly wooded. In fact, the further away from the ravine they went, the fewer the trees became. The river that had flowed so fiercely through the ravine now meandered leisurely at the bottom of the valley, some eighty feet below the narrow track, twisting its way about halfway up the hillside.

The almost barren slopes offered no protection from attack except by its very openness. Surprise attack by anyone was completely out of the question. Brogan felt quite safe in such surroundings.

'Have you noticed that we is headin' south again?' Brogan observed. 'Quite a change in the countryside too.'

'For some reason I don't know,' said Pete. 'This side o' the hills never gets much rain. Some know-all feller from England did explain why it was, but I don't reckon anyone ever understood.' He looked ahead with interest. 'See that ridge up ahead? I can't be certain, but I kinda recognize that big rock on top. If I'm right, the mines are not far on the other side.'

'How far do you reckon?'

'If I'm right, I'd say maybe three miles at most but we gotta get outa this valley.'

'Looks easy enough,' said Brogan. 'What's the other side of that ridge?'

'Another valley,' said Pete. 'But that's the one we wanna be in. I'd say we gotta try at that ridge.'

'It's about a mile to the ridge,' said Brogan. 'We've got company again!' He nodded to the far side of the valley. 'They've been with us for about half an hour. They won't try nothin' here though, even one gun could give 'em too much trouble out here.'

Pete shaded his eyes and looked at the top of the hills. 'I don't see nobody,' he said. 'I guess I'll have to take your word for it. You ain't been wrong yet, so I reckon you ain't wrong now.'

'They'll probably leave it till we're out of this valley,' said Brogan. 'What's the valley like over the ridge?'

'Wider'n flatter'n this one if I remember right,' said Pete. 'I only seen it from the camp though, you understand.'

'Trees? Rocks?' prompted Brogan.

'Plenty of rocks,' said Pete. 'Don't remember no trees.'

'I'd say that was where they'll ambush us.'

'You don't seem all that bothered about it,' said Pete.

'I ain't!' Brogan laughed.

Pete shook his head. 'Don't understand you at all. You go to all this trouble an' suddenly you ain't bothered.'

'Stayin' alive is the only thing I'm bothered about,' said Brogan. 'C'mon, let's get a move on an' get over that ridge.'

Pete's mule, Esmerelda, obstinately refused to be rushed. The most she could be coaxed into was a slightly faster than usual walk. The ridge was reached without incident and in fact proved to be a natural barrier which diverted the valley eastward. The side of the ridge comprised of loose scree, but it was not too difficult to climb and a quarter of an hour later they were at the top, looking down into a wide, flat bottomed valley with no trees and not even any sizable rocks which would offer any cover.

Pete pointed to the far end of the straight valley. 'See that old buildin' right up against the rock face at the far end?' Brogan nodded. 'That's an old winch house. There's a couple of disused mines just there. The main camp is about half of mile away from it.'

'An' from here to there looks like about two miles,' said Brogan. He studied the hills on the other side of the valley they had just left. 'It could be they is already up ahead,' he said. 'The couple that was watchin' us have gone. They must know we've gotta cross here. Yeh, I reckon we is gonna have a reception committee.'

'We could hide the money again,' suggested
Pete. 'We could get a party from the camp to come
back an' collect it.'

'I don't reckon they'll fall for that one twice!'
Brogan laughed. 'They find we ain't got it, all they
do is search back an' they'll find it. We've been
under observation almost all the time remember,
an' they know we've got the money. No, this time I
reckon we've just got to trust to luck.'

Pete looked at the layout of the land ahead and
was forced to agree that luck was going to have to
play a large part if they were to succeed. They
slithered down the slope to the firmer bed of the
valley and immediately headed as fast as they
could, although Brogan was restricted by the
speed of Pete's mule, for the mining camp.
Although Pete did manage to urge Esmerelda into
something like a gallop, it did not last long and
she soon reduced speed to her usual steady plod.

'Thought they would be!' Brogan grunted.

'Thought who would be?' queried Pete.

'Indians an' half-breeds!' said Brogan. 'About
three hundred yards ahead an' closin' fast.'

'I can't even see 'em, let alone hear 'em!'
complained Pete, shielding his eyes from the glare
of the sun.

'It's an old trick,' said Brogan. 'Allus attack with
the sun behind you.' He saw Pete reach for his
rifle. 'I wouldn't bother if I was you, you'd more'n
like be dead 'fore you could draw it.'

Pete looked at Brogan in amazement. 'You

mean you is just gonna let 'em take the money?'
Brogan nodded. 'Man! I don't understand you at
all. You've risked your life gettin' this close an'
now you're simply gonna hand it over to 'em
without a fight?'

'Like I say,' said Brogan, with a wry smile, 'I
know when I'm beat an' stayin' alive is more
important than all the money there is as far as I'm
concerned.'

'Well I ain't gonna give in so easy!' Pete snarled.
'You just cover me while I ride for the camp!' He
urged Esmerelda into a gallop and the mule ran
hard for about fifty yards and then stopped
completely. Very quickly he was surrounded by
the Indians who were laughing loudly at his feeble
effort. Brogan too was surrounded, but they were
not as casual with him as they were with Pete.
Three of them had their rifles aimed steadily at
his belly.

'I salute you!' The Indian leader smiled and
nodded at Brogan. 'I do not know even now how
you managed to get by us with the money and I do
not think you will tell me. You are an unusual
man for a white man, you seem to know almost as
much about bushcraft as we do.'

'I'd say I know more'n you,' said Brogan. 'I been
around a lot longer. You're still wet behind the
ears!'

'Your insults mean nothing!' The Indian
laughed. 'All your knowledge and trickery have
achieved you nothing!' He held up the satchel.
'See, it is we who have the money, so who has the

greater knowledge?'

Brogan smiled. 'Can't argue with that. OK, you've won!'

'I hope you realize that you've probably taken the last payroll you is ever gonna take, Red Wolf ... ' That was the first time Brogan had heard the Indian's name. 'After this Mitchell is gonna send a whole load of armed men.'

'We know our time is come,' said Red Wolf. 'It has been good while it lasted. We move on to new lands.'

'That'll mean goin' even further off the reservation,' said Pete. 'Why don't you make peace with your people instead of teamin' up with trash like them?' He nodded at the two white men.

'These are our lands!' snarled Red Wolf. 'But you are white, you would not understand. I agree with you the others are trash, along with my brothers from the tribe, I will leave them, all of them! However, that is no problem of yours. Your problem is to tell Mitchell what has happened!' He raised the satchel again with a cry of triumph. 'Go now, we have no wish to harm you, but I am not so certain about Mr Mitchell. He will not be very pleased with you.'

He rode off at speed for the safety of the hills and the others followed, whooping with delight. Brogan did not hang about and urged his horse forward.

'What you in such a darned hurry for?' demanded Pete.

'I just wanna get this over with,' said Brogan.

'Don't see what you gotta worry about, 'ceptin' you won't get your two hundred dollars.'

'I'll get my money!' said Brogan, with a broad grin.

Pete shook his head. 'Don't figure you at all! I only hope you know what you're doin', for your own sake. Mr Mitchell ain't a man to be taken lightly.'

'Nor am I,' said Brogan. 'I reckon Mitchell an' me know each other pretty well. Maybe he knew more than I gave him credit for.'

'There you go again, talkin' in riddles!' moaned Pete.

Brogan simply smiled and rode on and eventually they arrived at the mining camp, where they were met by the foreman, Jim Harker and his assistant, Steve Bates. The one thing that did surprise Brogan, although there was no real reason, was that all the miners appeared to be Chinese. Chinese workers were quite common on the railroads and he had come across them employed in mines before. His surprise was due more to the fact that up to then nobody had even mentioned the fact.

'You finally made it then?' Jim Harker grumbled. 'We weren't sure if you was ever goin' to arrive or not. I guess you must've had a long detour since you're comin' from that direction.'

'We made it!' Pete growled. 'The payroll didn't though.'

'Red Wolf?' asked Harker, not appearing to be very surprised.

'Red Wolf!' confirmed Pete. 'We got within about two miles an' Brogan here just let 'em take it!'

'Mr Mitchell ain't gonna be too pleased with you,' said Bates. 'You was hired to get it through.'

'I wasn't hired to get myself killed,' Brogan pointed out, 'but I am kinda curious. How the hell did you know I'd been hired by Mitchell? There ain't no way you could've known.'

Steve Bates looked nervously and quickly at Harker. 'Yeh, well, obvious ain't it? You come in with Pete.'

'That don't mean a thing,' said Brogan. 'We could've met up anywhere.'

'Yeh, well, we just knew,' said Harker. 'Anyhow, it's you what's got some explainin' to do, not us.'

'I've got nothin' to explain,' said Brogan. 'I'd say it was Mitchell who'd got the explainin' to do.'

'Will someone please tell me what the hell's goin' on?' demanded Pete. 'First of all you start talkin' in riddles back there an' now it looks like they knew you was hired when they shouldn't've done. There's a bunch of Indians an' half-breeds out there with a sizable wad of money. Shouldn't we all be goin' after 'em?'

'Are you gonna tell him, Harker,' said Brogan, 'or shall we let Mitchell tell him?'

'Tell me what?' screamed Pete. 'What the hell's goin' on? Nobody never tells me nothin'!'

Jim Harker looked at Brogan and smiled. 'How'd you figure it out?'

'I just got kinda curious,' said Brogan. 'That satchel was child's play to get in without breakin' the seal.'

Pete threw up his arms in despair. 'I give up! Will someone please tell me?'

'All Red Wolf got this time was a wad of paper!' Brogan laughed.

'Paper!' exclaimed Pete.

'Yeh, paper!' said Brogan. 'You can come out an' explain it yourself, Mitchell. I know you're in that hut!'

'You seem to know a lot of things, McNally!' Mitchell came out of the hut. 'How did you know I was in there?'

'Most folk don't wear fancy boots,' said Brogan. ''Specially when they is workin'. I could see 'em under the door. 'Sides, that's your horse over there.'

'Very observant!' Mitchell nodded. 'Yes, Pete, I am afraid you have been escorting a worthless bundle of paper.'

'Paper!' exclaimed Pete. 'You mean you almost had us killed for nothin' but paper?'

Mitchell laughed. 'It seemed to be the obvious way to get the money through.'

'Why the hell didn't you tell us?' demanded Pete.

'It was essential that you thought it was the payroll. If you'd known you'd probably have given up earlier. When did you find out, McNally?'

'Last night,' admitted Brogan. 'I guessed we was goin' to have trouble so I was goin' to take the money out of the satchel an' hide it under my shirt. That seal of yours ain't no good at all, I got in easy enough without breakin' it.'

'Let me get this thing straight!' said Pete. 'You mean you let us risk our lives carryin' worthless paper just so's you could bring the payroll through?' Everyone nodded. 'Hell! That's just about the meanest, most low-down trick I ever heard! We could've gotten ourselves killed.'

'Personally I thought it was a darned good idea,' said Mitchell. 'As for you gettin' killed, it wouldn't have made no difference if the money was in the bag or not. This way the bandits spent all their time chasin' you, leavin' me to take the easy route in peace and even if they had seen me they probably wouldn't have thought anything of it. They must know I go up to the mines sometimes.'

'I gotta be gettin' old!' Brogan said, with a wry smile. 'I shoulda seen it comin'. I remember thinkin' that it didn't make sense to risk that kinda money, but I gotta admit I never thought about it at the time.'

'An' how do you feel about the possibility of bein' killed for some worthless bits of paper?' asked Jim Harker.

Brogan shrugged. 'If'n I'd been killed, it wouldn't've been of no interest to me if it was a sack of diamonds, I sure wouldn't've known anythin' about it. Dead is dead an' I ain't never met a dead man yet what needed any money.'

'Well I think it was a shit thing to do!' hissed Pete.

'You'll get your usual pay,' said Mitchell. 'I might even be feelin' a bit generous an' give you a bonus.' Pete immediately brightened up at the prospect. 'I haven't decided yet, but I'll think about it. As for your money, McNally, you'll have to go back to Abbotsville for it. I don't carry that kind of money about in loose change.'

'That's the way I was headed in the first place,' said Brogan. 'Are we gonna ride back together?'

'What's the matter, don't you trust me to go back to town?' asked Mitchell.

'I don't reckon I'd trust you with a baby's wooden rattle!' said Brogan, sincerely but with a smile.

'Then you can either go on ahead yourself or wait here for me. I'll be at least two days. I want to see what this new seam is like.'

'I'll rest up for the day an' start back in the mornin',' said Brogan. 'I prefer travellin' by myself, it's a lot less bother. Other folks usually seem to end up in trouble.'

'Suit yourself,' said Mitchell. He slapped Pete across the shoulders. 'Sorry about what I did, but it was just about the only way I was goin' to guarantee the payroll gettin' through.'

'You could've just as easy been robbed yourself!' Pete pointed out. 'Maybe even killed. Would've taught you a lesson if'n you had been killed!'

'But I wasn't!' Mitchell said, laughing at Pete's logic.

'There's plenty of grub in the cookhouse!' invited Steve Bates. 'Just tell the cook I sent you.'

'Thanks,' said Brogan. 'I am kinda hungry.'

'So am I, but I don't like Chinky food,' complained Pete. 'A man never knows just what

he's eatin' when it's all chopped up like that. I like
to see what I'm eatin'!'

'There's proper food there too,' assured Mitchell.
'I don't like Chinese food either.'

'Don't bother me what I eat!' said Brogan.

'He's right too,' exclaimed Pete. 'You know what
he ate last night? Lizard an' funny onion things!'

'You ate it too,' Brogan pointed out.

'I guess a man'll eat anythin' if he's hungry
enough!' muttered Pete. 'Even Chinky food!'

'Since when have you been particular about
food?' asked Mitchell. 'I've never known you
refuse it, 'specially when it's free.'

'That don't mean to say I gotta like it,' muttered
Pete.

There was 'proper food' in the cookhouse in the
form of large steaks. Both Brogan and Pete opted
for one each, topped with three eggs and washed
down with a large mug of very strong coffee.
Afterwards, Brogan wandered about the site for a
while before stretching himself out in the shade of
a tree until sundown.

'I could still use you!'

Brogan looked up and blinked. 'I ain't for hire. I
thought I made that much plain.'

Mitchell laughed slightly. 'Yeh, you made it
plain. I've never met a man like you before. Most
men would work for me a while until they got
some money behind 'em an' then move on.'

'When you've paid me, I shall have some
money,' Brogan pointed out. 'An' I shall be movin'
on.'

'Two hundred dollars ain't that much,' said Mitchell, sitting alongside Brogan and sniffing pointedly. 'God! You do smell!'

'That's another reason you wouldn't want me workin' for you,' Brogan said with a grin.

'It's nothin' soap an' hot water can't cure,' said Mitchell.

'Mister!' sighed Brogan. 'You just gave the one reason why I could never work for nobody, they'd all expect me to have a bath. I'll face a gunman any day an' think nothin' of it, but the very mention of soap an' hot water an' I run a mile. Bathin' ain't healthy an' it ain't natural.'

Mitchell laughed. 'OK, I reckon I could even put up with you stinkin'. The offer still stands.'

Brogan sniffed at his sleeve. 'I don't smell that bad, can't do after havin' that all over soak in the river. That's gotta count as a bath.'

'Yeh, Pete told me about that,' said Mitchell. 'You sure took a chance, you could easily have been drowned.'

'Drowned or shot, dead is still dead!'

'I guess so,' agreed Mitchell. 'So where you headed once you leave Abbotsville?'

'Wherever takes my fancy,' said Brogan.

'It seems a pretty pointless life. Don't you ever get bored with it? Just wanderin' from place to place don't seem like no kinda life to me.'

'Bored?' Brogan thought for a moment. 'No, can't say as I've ever been bored. No two days are the same, no two places are the same an' I can assure you I've had enough excitement in my life to satisfy most men several times over.'

'You still need money though,' said Mitchell, 'even you admit that much.' Brogan nodded. 'Accordin' to your reckonin' I owe you two hundred dollars. ... '

'Two hundred an' fifty!' Brogan corrected.

'Two hundred an' fifty?'

'Like all businessmen, you got a mighty short memory when it suits you,' said Brogan. 'Two fifty is what we agreed.'

'Yeh, well, OK,' nodded Mitchell.

'I guess I disappointed you,' said Brogan. 'I reckon you was hopin' Pete an' me'd get killed, that way it wouldn't've cost you nothin'.'

Mitchell grinned. 'I guess it would have done at that! I've got to admit I certainly wouldn't've lost no sleep or shed no tears for either of you. Two hundred an' fifty! Just supposin' I decide not to pay you. Just what the hell could you do about it?'

Brogan studied Mitchell's face for a moment. 'Just supposin' you was to end up dead!'

'You'd go that far?' Mitchell laughed, but he was not at all sure of himself.

'You prepared to find out?'

'No, I guess not,' admitted Mitchell. 'OK, you can either wait an' go back with me or you can go ahead an' wait.'

'I already said I'll go on ahead,' said Brogan.

'Fine with me,' said Mitchell. 'It's just about chow time, you comin'?'

'Two meals in one day!' Brogan laughed. 'I ain't used to that kinda thing. Might as well make the most of it while I can I reckon.' He followed Mitchell to the cookhouse and sat down to another steak, this time served with vegetables and potatoes.

Mitchell and his two foremen sat apart from Brogan and Pete and Brogan was conscious that he appeared to be the topic of conversation. It did not bother him unduly, but he did wonder what they were saying about him. Nothing untoward happened for the remainder of the evening, apart from Pete deciding to finish off his 'comfort'. Brogan was offered a bed in a cabin, but declined, preferring to sleep in the open alongside his horse. Besides, he felt slightly uneasy and felt safer out in the open.

EIGHT

Brogan had considered leaving before dawn, but he decided that a free breakfast was well worth waiting for, especially since it was a luxury he did not have the chance of very often. It also seemed rather pointless to make a very early start since he would have to wait in Abbotsville for Mitchell.

Breakfast consisted of hash and coffee which, while quite welcome to Brogan, seemed rather unpopular with the others, especially Jim Harker who complained that breakfast always consisted of hash and coffee. Harker's assistant, Steve Bates, was not present at the meal.

'I heard him ride out last night,' said Brogan. 'Seems a funny time to go anywhere to me.'

'Yeh … well … ' faltered Mitchell, 'He should've gone earlier in the day. He had to ride to the railhead an' make arrangements for the ore to be shipped out.'

'Railroad?' queried Brogan. 'How far's that? I didn't see no sign of any railroad when I rode through.'

'About thirty miles due east,' said Harker. 'He

110

had to be there at first light this mornin', that's when the freight manager gets there.'

'How the hell do you get the ore to the railroad?' asked Brogan.

Mitchell pointed beyond a heap of rock. 'Wagons! There's about twenty of 'em. We make a run about once every two weeks.'

'It'd make more sense if the railroad was to come here,' said Brogan.

'Oh, they'll put a line up here all right.' Mitchell laughed. 'At my expense. I can't afford the kinda money they're talkin' about, not yet anyhow, maybe in the future.'

'I guess you know your own business!' Brogan shrugged. He was not entirely satisfied with the explanation of Steve Bates riding out late at night, partly because he felt it most unlikely that special arrangements would have to be made every time ore was shipped out, but mainly because he knew that Bates had gone in the opposite direction – towards Abbotsville! He was tempted to make it known that he knew, but something told him that he would be wasting his time. Steve Bates had ridden towards Abbotsville, of that he was certain and he was equally certain neither Harker nor Mitchell would tell him the truth.

Pete had decided that he too was not going to wait for Mitchell and, a little to Brogan's dismay, appeared with his mule just as Brogan was about to ride out.

'Ain't much point in me hangin' around here,' said Pete. 'Mind if I join you?'

'You got a right to go where you want when you want,' said Brogan. 'Just like me.'

'Which means you ain't too keen on my company,' grunted Pete. 'That's OK, I prefer my own company anyhow.'

Brogan sighed, realizing that he was being a little too hard on the old man. 'Didn't mean no offence,' he said. 'Sure, you can ride with me, we shouldn't have no trouble on the way back.'

'Maybe we will, maybe we won't,' said Pete. 'I wouldn't be too sure about that.'

'What you mean by that?' asked Brogan.

'Just keep on goin' an' don't look back!' hissed Pete.

Brogan knew when to ask questions and when not to ask and he kept a straight face and rode on, slightly ahead of the old man. When they were climbing up the trail behind the mine and out of sight of everyone below, he stopped to allow Pete and his mule to catch up.

'OK!' he said. 'What was all that about?'

'Steve Bates didn't ride down to the railroad,' said Pete. 'I know, I overheard him an' Mitchell talkin'.'

'I know he didn't,' said Brogan. 'He headed for Abbotsville!'

Pete looked at Brogan with a wry smile. 'I shoulda guessed you'd know. Why didn't you say anythin' to Mitchell?'

'What for?' asked Brogan. 'They wouldn't've told the truth, you know that. I know he didn't head for the railroad, that's all that matters to me.'

'An' don't it bother you why?' asked Pete.

'More'n like he's been sent on ahead to kill me, an' you, now you've decided to come along.'

'You treat it very casual,' said Pete. 'Yeh, it could be one reason, but somehow I got me this feelin' it ain't entirely that. Steve Bates ain't no gunman an' as far as I know he ain't no killer either. He can be a real mean bastard with them Chinks, but I don't rate him as a killer.'

'Well, we gotta assume he's been sent ahead to kill me,' said Brogan. 'That way I'll be on the lookout for trouble.'

'An' why should Mitchell want you dead?' asked Pete.

'It'd save him two hundred an' fifty dollars,' Brogan pointed out. 'Men have been killed for less.'

'Two hundred an' fifty? Naw, Mitchell wouldn't soil his hands for that little.'

'So what did you overhear 'em talkin' about?'

'Nothin' much,' admitted Pete. 'I just heard Mitchell tell him to make sure they knew when it was due an' to make sure they weren't recognized.'

'Who the hell are "they" an' what's due?'

'Hanged if I know!' Pete shrugged. 'But I do know one thing, Mitchell is in deep trouble with the bank an' I also know he never brought no money up to the mine.'

'How'd you know all that?' asked Brogan.

'Bout the money he shoulda brought to the mine? Easy, but I don't expect someone like you to've spotted it!' Pete grinned triumphantly. 'Chinese is just about the biggest gamblers in the world. They play the weird game they call mahjong, or somethin' like that. Did you see any sign of gamblin' last night?'

'I saw a few of 'em playin' for pennies,' said Brogan, 'but no big money as far as I could see.'

'Exactly!' gloated Pete, very pleased that he had got one up on Brogan. 'If they'd been paid most of 'em would've been bettin' their entire wages. That's how they are, seem to live for nothin' else but workin' an' gamblin'. Most of 'em don't realize it, but they're bein' cheated all the time. There's about three Chinks what are really powerful, they don't work in the mine, they make their money by lendin' to the others, chargin' huge interest, as well as makin' sure they lose what they got left at gamblin'. They keep Harker an' Bates happy with a sweetener, so everyone's happy.'

'I allus said you're never too old to learn!' Brogan laughed. 'Don't know if that kinda information will ever be any use to me, but I'll remember. OK, so the money never reached the mine. What happened to it an' why?'

'Like I said!' Pete smiled. 'I know Mitchell's in deep trouble with the banks. I heard they was threatenin' to call in their mortgage, which means Mitchell will have to give up his land.'

'How'd you know all that?'

'Nobody takes any notice of a drunk!' Pete laughed. 'I overheard Mitchell an' Evans, the bank president, talkin' the other mornin'. Mr

Evans told Mitchell that this was goin' to be the last time he'd let him have any money for anythin'. Mitchell was to tell the miners they was bein' laid off as soon as they was paid. After that, Mitchell had two weeks to come up with fifty thousand or he would foreclose.'

'Fifty thousand!' exclaimed Brogan. 'Surely he's got that much?'

'Not in cash!' Pete grinned. 'That two thousand for the payroll was the bank's money, not Mitchell's. I reckon he hit on the idea of takin' the payroll after you saved it for him. You an' me is hired to bring it up here, we gets robbed on the way an' if we gets killed, that's a bonus.'

'But we know the money was never in that bag,' Brogan pointed out. ''Sides, it was Evans who handed the bag over.'

'Yeh, that had me for a while too,' admitted Pete. 'But if you remember, it was Mitchell who carried it out the bank. He musta made a switch somehow.'

'I must admit I didn't take too much notice,' said Brogan. 'OK, so somehow, Mitchell switched bags. When I told him I knew it was only paper, after we'd been robbed, he didn't have much choice but to admit it and pretend he'd brought the money. I guess that means both Harker an' Evans was paid to keep quiet. He rides out to the mine just in case we make it through without bein' robbed an' arranges with Bates to have us killed on the way back an' then tell Evans we was robbed an' killed.'

'I agree with all of that,' said Pete. ''Ceptin' the

part where Bates is goin' to kill us. I still don't buy
that.'

'Then what?' asked Brogan.

'More to the point,' said Pete, 'who did Bates go
to see an' what is it that's due?'

'That's the least of our problems,' said Brogan.
'If what we've just been sayin' is all true, Mitchell
can't afford to let us get back to Abbotsville. He
tried buyin' me off by offerin' me a job, but he
could see I wasn't havin' none of that, so the next
logical step is to kill me. Whatever else he's got
planned, killin' me has got to be high on his list.'

'An' how about me?' asked Pete. 'I knew what
was goin' on too!'

'Then he either has you killed as well or he buys
you off. Personally I reckon he could've bought
you off.'

'I have got certain principles!' objected Pete.

'An' one of 'em is a dedication to whisky!'
Brogan sneered. 'The promise of an endless
supply would've soon satisfied your principles.'

Pete huffed but did not try to deny it. 'I still
don't reckon Bates has got what it takes to kill a
man!'

'He's got a gun!' Brogan pointed out. 'I know
what you mean though. Some folk find it easy to
squeeze that trigger but most folks find they can't
do it when there's another human bein' in their
sights.'

'I'd say you was one of those who found it easy!'
said Pete, very quietly. 'Almost too easy I'd say.'

Brogan thought for a few moments. 'Sure, I can

kill when I've got to an' think nothin' of it, but I try not to kill anyone unless I've got to. That kinda killin' is bad!'

Pete suddenly snatched at his gun as something crashed through the undergrowth at the side of the trail. 'Deer! Hell, McNally, you've got me all jittery!'

'Better to be jittery an' alive than all calm an' dead!' Brogan laughed. 'Don't worry, I don't reckon anyone is goin' to try nothin' yet awhile, we're too close to the mine.'

'Strikes me you is all calm!' muttered Pete. 'Too bloody calm!'

'I'm ready though!' assured Brogan.

As Brogan had predicted, the first part of their journey was quiet and they made slow but steady progress. It was towards dusk when Brogan suddenly called a halt, motioned to Pete to remain silent, and listened intently.

'Shootin'!' he said, eventually.

'I didn't hear nothin',' said Pete.

'I did,' replied Brogan, 'it was shootin' all right!'

'An' just who the hell would be shootin' at who?' demanded Pete.

'I can hear a lot of things,' said Brogan, sarcastically, 'but even I can't tell who's shootin' who.'

'OK, so what do we do?' asked Pete. 'I'll take your word for it, you ain't been wrong so far.'

'There ain't that much we can do,' said Brogan. 'Just be ready, that's all.'

'It's probably them renegades an' half-breeds,'

said Pete. 'Maybe they jumped somebody who tried shootin' back.'

'Could be,' agreed Brogan, 'but I guess the only way to find out is to keep on goin'.'

'Keep on goin', the man says!' sighed Pete. 'OK, we all got to die sometime I suppose.'

They made very slow progress for the next hour, covering a distance of little more than two miles, when Brogan stopped again and indicated that Pete should hide. Pete took his mule and Brogan's horse into some thick brush and Brogan disappeared on foot.

There was nothing to see, at least not to the untrained eye, but to Brogan the signs screamed out messages of recent and bloody conflict. He scouted the area around the hollow and found little trace of anything except the clear signs of horses having passed through in the direction of Abbotsville very recently. With all the other horse tracks, it was impossible to say exactly how many there were. Some of the tracks were obviously made by Indian ponies, in fact they made up the majority. It was easy to tell which they were since they did not have any horseshoes. Intermingled with these were other tracks with horseshoes.

He returned to the hollow and looked around. He was troubled, something was wrong and he did not know what. There were no obvious signs which made him think all was not as it seemed – just a gut feeling and he had long since learned never to disregard his gut feelings – they had never proved him wrong yet.

The signs of violence were everywhere; trampled, muddy grass, broken branches, scattered leaves, sliding hoof prints and even a couple of bullets lodged in a tree trunk. It was not these signs which bothered him, these he would have expected – there was something else.

He returned to Pete and told him what he had found and Pete seemed quite unimpressed, stating that it was quite obvious that one party or the other had taken off in pursuit of the other. Brogan was still unhappy about something and began a more detailed search of the area. Pete thought he was quite mad but took the opportunity to make camp for the night.

Brogan's persistence paid off – rather gruesomely. The first indication was a crow hopping noisily away from the branches of a fallen tree. The tree was plainly only recently fallen, its canopy of green still intact. More out of curiosity than anything else, Brogan examined the stump of the tree and it seemed quite obvious that its fall was due to having been felled than by natural means. This struck Brogan as rather strange, people did not normally chop trees down just for the sake of it.

He walked the length of the trunk and peered among its fallen branches. At first he could see nothing but eventually he was able to make out what appeared to be the bodies of several men, apparently naked. He pulled the branches further apart and two bodies could be seen quite plainly.

'Pete!' he called. 'I think I found your Indian friends, or what's left of 'em!'

'What you mean, what's left of 'em?' grumbled Pete as he joined Brogan and peered down among the branches as Brogan held them up. 'Jeez!' Pete gasped. 'Are they all there?'

'There's seven I can see plain enough,' said Brogan, 'an' I reckon there's another one over there.' He pointed. 'I'd say they was all here.'

'An' all naked?'

'Looks like it,' said Brogan.

'What they all naked for?' asked Pete.

'How the hell should I know that?' Brogan laughed.

'You just gonna leave 'em there?' asked Pete.

'You want 'em out, you get 'em out!' replied Brogan, letting the branches fall back into place. 'One thing's certain, whoever put 'em there sure didn't want 'em found.'

'Mitchell!' sneered Pete.

'Everythin' sure seems to come back to him,' agreed Brogan. 'Somebody's sure goin' to a hell of a lot of trouble. Why should they wanna kill the renegades an' then, havin' killed 'em, why go to all the trouble of hidin' the fact? I'm darned sure if they'd killed 'em an' told the sheriff they'd more'n like've been rewarded.'

'Why they was killed is easy,' said Pete, rather triumphantly. 'Red Wolf an' his men were the only other folk who knew that satchel was only stuffed with paper an' Mitchell can't afford for anyone he can't trust to know.'

'They was renegades an' outlaws,' reminded Brogan. 'Nobody would've believed them.'

'Maybe Mitchell warn't prepared to take the chance,' said Pete. 'Somebody might've believed 'em an' started askin' awkward questions.'

'Yeh, I can see why they had to be killed,' said Brogan, 'but it still don't make sense to hide the bodies an' even less sense to strip 'em naked.'

'Nothin' don't make sense no more!' grumbled Pete.

'I can't help feelin' that it all seems one hell of a waste of time,' said Brogan. 'Not for two thousand dollars. I could undertstand it for the fifty thousand the bank wants, but not two thousand.'

'Who's to know how a man like Mitchell thinks!' Pete shrugged. 'You reckon Red Wolf an' his boys were ambushed an' I say if they were, Mitchell was behind it. Don't expect me to know the reason why, an' right now I couldn't care less.'

'Why's that?'

'Obvious ain't it?' Pete scorned. 'We're both marked men. You don't think Mitchell is gonna just let us go do you? If you've got a lick of sense at all, you'll get the hell out of it right now an' forget all about your money. I reckon it's about the only thing either of us can do. If we stay in Abbotsville it's a sure fire bet that we're gonna meet with some kinda accident.'

'Could be you is right!' agreed Brogan. 'I'll think about it.'

'Think about it!' exclaimed Pete. 'I reckon you must have some kind of death wish! I know I ain't goin' nowhere near Abbotsville.'

'That's your choice,' said Brogan. 'Me, I don't

take kindly to bein' made a fool of by no man. I've got to find out what the hell Mitchell is up to.'

'Even if it kills you?'

'Dead is dead no matter what,' said Brogan, 'an' we all gotta die sometime I reckon.'

'I'd like to think I had a bit longer to live,' said Pete, 'an' I sure ain't about to invite anyone to kill me. It ain't worth it, no town an' no man is worth the risk.'

'I suppose I agree with that,' said Brogan, 'but I guess I'm just curious – nosey, some folk would call it.'

'Stupid is what I call it!' responded Pete.

Brogan let the subject drop for a while and sat pondering about what it all meant. He was still quite convinced that what had happened so far was far too elaborate for just two thousand dollars, there had to be more to it. He wandered back to the fallen tree and peered among the branches.

'Forget it!' he said to himself. 'It ain't none of your business an' it ain't worth the risk.'

'We need the money,' he replied to himself.

'An' you reckon you're gonna get it?'

'No, don't look like it,' he was forced to agree.

'OK, so call it a day an' do like Pete, get the hell out of it.'

'I'd just like to know what's goin' on.'

'That's your problem, you always want to know what's goin' on. You was right, you are bloody nosey an' it's gonna be the death of you one day.'

'Yeh, maybe you're right!'

His little talk with himself had resolved nothing, it rarely did, but it usually made him feel better. He returned to the fire and huddled in front of it. It was now quite dark but he did not expect any trouble that night.

'Ain't you got any idea what Mitchell an' Bates was talkin' about?' he asked Pete.

'Nope!' replied Pete, firmly. 'Don't want to know either.'

'Seems plain to me that somethin' else is afoot. Why else should he tell Bates to make sure they weren't recognized an' make sure they knew when it was due? What's due an' when?'

'It's all too much for a simple feller like me,' said Pete.

'What's due, an' when?' Brogan mused, ignoring his elderly companion. 'Are you sure you didn't hear nothin' about somethin' bein' delivered to Abbotsville?'

'I'm sure,' replied Pete. 'If there had been somethin' special on I reckon I would've heard about it. Nope, there's nothin'. Nothin' much ever happens in Abbotsville anyhow. Highlight of the week is the stage in either direction on Tuesday's an' Thursdays.'

'Stage?' Brogan queried. 'Normal passenger stage or freight?'

Pete looked at him rather strangely. 'Bit of both I suppose. There ain't usually many passengers, maybe three at the most. Come to think of it, there is another regular monthly wagon, carryin' goods for the general store an' such like. That comes through 'bout once a month, but I don't think it has a regular day.'

'When's that due?'

Pete thought for a moment. 'Naw, that can't be it. That came through a couple of days before you arrived, so there ain't another due for at least four weeks.'

'You say the stage comes through on Tuesdays and Thursdays? What day is it today?'

'Wednesday – I think!'

Brogan had to think for a few minutes. 'Yeh, I reckon it is. Don't normally bother what day it is, it don't matter none usually.'

'I see what you're thinkin'!' said Pete. 'Whoever Bates went to see, they're gonna hold up the stage. Could be, but what the hell for? It don't carry nothin' but people an' mail an' the odd parcel. It sure don't carry gold or money, leastways not as far as I know.'

'Well there ain't nothin' else that makes sense in all this,' said Brogan.

'Which is why it's best left alone!' said Pete, solemnly.

NINE

Reason and common sense told Brogan to forget the whole thing and carry on as if nothing had ever happened, but, he was not like that. He was quite capable of ignoring a situation, which he had done on many occasions, but once he had become involved he almost always wanted to see it through, no matter what the dangers were. This was the case with Mitchell and his money and exactly what was due.

'This stage what's due,' he said to Pete, the following morning. 'Which way does it come?'

'East,' replied Pete. 'Tuesdays is from the West headin' east and Thursdays is from the east headin' west.'

'East!' mused Brogan. 'That means it's gotta cross these hills somewhere don't it?'

'I'd say about thirty miles north of where we are now,' replied Pete. 'It's about the narrowest place an' not too steep either.'

'Ideal for anyone what wanted to rob it?'

'Good a place as any,' agreed Pete, 'it's been done before, not recently, but it has been robbed.

Last time musta been about six months ago. Come to think of it that was on the other stage, not that it matters that much, they've both been hit.'

'So it wouldn't be too much of a surprise if it was robbed again?' Brogan observed.

'I guess not,' agreed Pete. 'There ain't normally anythin' worth takin' 'ceptin' what the travellers got on them, although they usually take the parcels an' things. If they don't reckon the parcels contain anythin' worth keepin', we usually find 'em scattered along the trail somewheres.'

'Was it usually a regular gang who held it up?'

'Naw, drifters like you mainly. They caught the last two an' strung 'em up. They reckon Red Wolf held it up once, but I don't buy that, it ain't his style an' it'd only invite trouble he could do without.'

'It won't buy him no more trouble,' said Brogan. Suddenly he sat up bolt upright. 'That's it!'

'That's what?'

'Red Wolf!' exclaimed Brogan. 'That's why they was killed an' why they've been stripped naked an' buried under that tree! Whoever killed 'em wants everyone to think that Red Wolf robbed the stage! They're gonna dress up in their clothes.'

'Nice idea,' agreed Pete, 'an' it could just be, but as far as I'm concerned it's one more reason for not goin' back to Abbotsville. That kinda knowledge would definitely get a man killed an' I sure couldn't trust my mouth not to let me down after I'd had a few whiskies.'

'What time is the stage due in town?' asked Brogan.

'Usually arrives just about sundown,' said Pete.

'Then there's about another twelve hours!'

'If'n you say so,' muttered Pete. 'I don't know what you is plannin' but you is on your own. I told you, I'm givin' Abbotsville a wide berth.'

'Don't be in too much of a hurry,' said Brogan. 'OK, I'm on my own, I can't blame you for that. I don't know what I'm gonna do just yet, I gotta think about it. I'm ridin' on, I've gotta make time. I reckon you'll be all right on your own.'

'I'm a big boy!' Pete grinned. 'Since I ain't goin' back to town, it don't matter where I go or when. Sure, since you've set your mind on committin' suicide, go ahead, don't let me stand between you an' your Maker.'

Brogan rode out of the hollow and the hundred yards back onto the main trail and headed towards Abbotsville, He had twelve hours before the stage was due, less than that before it would pass through the hills. His first instinct was to keep on heading to where the stage crossed the hills, but he had no idea just how many men would be involved or exactly where they were. Even if he did locate them, it was doubtful if he could do anything to help the stage and then he might not be able to do anything. He decided to ride into Abbotsville and tell Sheriff Dempster all he knew and trust to luck that he was not part of the plan or in Mitchell's pay too deeply.

Five hours of hard riding brought him into Abbotsville and a rather surprised Sheriff

Dempster. The sheriff seemed slightly wary of Brogan's request to speak to him privately.

'I was just about to ride out to the Philips' ranch,' he objected, 'it'll have to wait.'

'It can't wait!' insisted Brogan. 'Not if you wanna stop the stage bein' robbed.'

The expression on Dempster's face was enough to tell Brogan that the sheriff knew nothing about what was happening – assuming that he was right.

'What you talkin' about?' demanded Dempster. 'Are you sayin' somebody's gonna rob the stage?'

'Wouldn't be the first time, would it?' said Brogan. 'That's exactly what I am sayin', Sheriff. Open your office an' I'll tell you all about it. It's all guesswork I know, but it's the only thing what makes sense.'

'OK, I'm listenin',' said Dempster, unlocking his office and inviting Brogan inside.

He listened intently and did not interrupt as Brogan explained what had happened and his theory about the likelihood of the stage being robbed.

'Sure sounds plausible enough,' admitted Dempster when Brogan had finished his story. 'An' I've got to agree with Pete about the miners an' gamblin', they'd've been straight at it as soon as they got their money. What don't make sense is holdin' up the stage coach, that's petty stuff, more the sort of thing someone like you would get up to, not Mitchell.'

'Thanks!' Brogan grinned. 'I ain't never robbed

nobody of nothin'. I agree though, it wouldn't make sense normally, but what if this time the stage is carryin' somethin' else, somethin' which would get Mitchell out of trouble?'

'Like what?'

'Money'd be the obvious thing,' replied Brogan.

'Could be,' admitted Dempster. 'I have known it carry cash from time to time, but never that much, four or five thousand at the most. I don't reckon that's it.'

'There is one man as'd know for sure,' said Brogan. 'The bank president, Evans. Even if he don't know, he'll be mighty interested in the stunt Mitchell pulled with the money.'

'I reckon he would too,' said Dempster. 'OK, let's go ask him!'

The sheriff led the way round to the bank and, after more or less ordering the clerk, who seemed to think that Mr Evans was higher than God and must never be disturbed, the man in question was summoned.

'I am a very busy man,' he objected to the sheriff. He looked at Brogan with extreme distaste. 'Am I to assume that your business also includes him?'

'I think you ought to listen to what he has to say,' said Dempster. 'It all sounds kinda wild, but I've got to admit it's convincin'.'

Evans looked around uneasily but finally had to admit defeat and invite the pair into his office, not inviting either of them to sit. Brogan however, sensing the animosity, gave him a broad grin and pulled up an expensive looking padded chair and sat down. Evans was too surprised to object.

'This had better be good!' he grunted, almost threateningly.

Once again Brogan explained what had happened and about his idea of the stage being robbed and, much to his and Sheriff Dempster's surprise, he did not pour scorn on the idea. Instead, he leant forward, almost confidentially.

'Are you quite certain about there being no money in the satchel? I can assure you there was more than two thousand dollars in it when I handed it over.'

'Couldn't be more certain,' replied Brogan. He took a piece of paper from his shirt pocket and handed it to Evans. 'It was all paper cut up like this. This is one of 'em.' Evans took the paper gingerly, as if expecting it to bite him, and examined it.

'It looks very much like a copy of our local weekly paper. Very well, Mr McNally, I accept your story so far. Now, what's all this about the stage being robbed?'

Once again Brogan explained his theory and once again Evans did not pour any scorn on the idea. When Brogan had finished, he sat back and stared up at the ceiling for quite some time.

'Is there any money comin' in on the stage?' asked the sheriff.

'Indeed there is,' sighed Evans. 'There should be two boxes, one for me and one for the bank in Black Rock.'

'Black Rock?' queried Brogan.

'The next town, about fifty miles west,' explained Dempster. 'Next stop for the stage.'

'Yes, two boxes,' mused Evans. 'The contents of the two should more than cover Mr Mitchell's debts, but there is something else which he would find even more valuable.'

'More valuable than all the money?' asked Brogan.

'Yes, much more,' said Evans. 'I am quite convinced that Mitchell does not know anything about the money, I know I have never mentioned it to him. Besides, apart from when I handed over the satchel, I have not seen him since I told him the bank was foreclosing. There is no way he could have known about the money.'

'Then just what the hell is it that's so important that he does know about?' asked Dempster.

'Deeds, Sheriff, deeds!'

'Deeds?' Brogan and the sheriff asked the question together.

'The deeds to his ranch and lands,' explained Evans. 'It is against bank rules to keep such documents in banks such as this, they are always held at head office. It is only in cases such as this that they ever leave head office vaults. Unfortunately they have to be available on the off chance that Mr Mitchell is able to find the fifty thousand he owes. If by some chance he is able to do so, I am required, by law, to have the deeds in my possession and hand them over on receipt of payment. Briefly, if I do not have the deeds, I cannot demand payment.'

'I get it,' said Brogan. 'He arranges for them deeds to be stolen, which means you can't foreclose.'

'It would certainly delay the process,' said Evans. 'Without the original documents it could take several years for the bank to prove its claim. They would undoubtedly be able to prove it, but it would give Mitchell a great deal of breathing space.'

'An' the money the stage is carryin' is a bonus for him,' said Brogan. 'Very nice too. It kinda makes sense now why he took the money meant for the miners. He's hired someone to rob the stage an' the money is to pay them since he don't know about the money on the stage. He might've guessed there'd be some, but he couldn't chance it. He had to have cash to pay them.'

'I would suggest that your powers of deduction have just about defined the situation exactly,' said Evans, for the first time showing a hint of a smile. 'Assuming that we have read the situation correctly, Sheriff, what is your next move?'

'I guess we've got to go meet the stage an' make sure it gets through,' he said. 'Ain't much else we can do.'

'We?' asked Brogan.

'I'll get a posse together,' said Dempster, 'but you've done all the work so far, I reckon you should be in on it.'

'I ain't so sure about that,' said Brogan. 'It ain't none of my concern what happens to Mitchell, the

stage or this town. So far it looks like I've done a
lot of work for nothin'. I saved the payroll an'
didn't get nothin' for it an' I made sure what
everyone thought was the payroll got through,
well almost, an' still I get nothin'. I know I'm only
a saddle tramp, but even folk like me need money.
I was promised two hundred an' fifty by Mitchell
to get the payroll through. I ain't so sure as I want
to risk my life for nothin' again.'

This time Mr Evans did break out in a broad
smile. 'Mr McNally, I think you are selling
yourself cheap at two hundred and fifty, but since
that amount would appear to satisfy your needs, I
am prepared to pay it to you, provided that you
help the sheriff see this thing through to a
successful conclusion.'

Brogan laughed. 'If I want the money, which I
do, I guess I've got no choice. You heard him,
Sheriff, he promised me!'

'I am a man of my word!' objected Evans. 'I have
not reached the position I have now by not
keeping my word. You will get your money,
providing Mitchell does not succeed.'

'Personally, I wouldn't trust a banker any
more'n I'd trust a buzzard not to eat a dead horse,'
said Brogan. 'OK, I'll go along with it, but I got
conditions too.'

'Conditions?' asked Evans.

'Yeh, one!' said Brogan. 'Your way it all depends
on Mitchell bein' stopped. Just supposin' we can't
stop him. Just supposin' the men he hired take
the stage before we think they will or somehow

the posse can't stop 'em. I still want somethin' to show for it.'

Evans looked seriously at Brogan. 'I must agree that you deserve something for what you have done thus far. Very well ... ' He reached into the drawer of his desk and took out five notes. 'Fifty dollars,' he continued. 'No matter what happens, this is yours ... ' He handed the money to Brogan. 'You get the other two hundred if you are successful. I shall need you to sign a receipt, your cross will do, Sheriff Dempster can witness it.'

'Thanks,' said Brogan, more than a little surprised. 'There ain't no need for nobody to witness nothin', I can read an' write.'

Evans looked quite surprised, but smiled again. 'I meant no disrespect. It is just that one does not expect the likes of you to be able to. Why do you live as you do if you can read and write?'

'Cos it suits me!' growled Brogan.

'If you say so,' said Evans, producing a sheet of paper on which he wrote the receipt and handed Brogan to sign. Satisfied with the signature, he dismissed both men with the wave of his hand.

'I'll get the posse together,' said Dempster, once they were outside. 'You hang about, I've got to swear you in too.'

'I had me a job as a sheriff, once,' said Brogan. 'Didn't take to it though. There ain't no need to swear me in, don't really see the point.'

'Don't see much point in it either,' said Dempster, 'but that's what I'm supposed to do. Besides, you'd be surprised how many folk expect it. They feel cheated if you don't. I can't force you I suppose.'

"Fore you go,' said Brogan, 'I been thinkin'. I know it'd probably be easier just to escort the stage here, but that'll mean you'd never be able to prove anythin' against Mitchell. Why not find where they are, tail 'em, let 'em start on the stage an' then move in an' catch 'em? That way you'd be sure to have someone who'd say it was Mitchell put 'em up to it. Believe me, they'll talk, 'specially if they think it'll do 'em some good.'

The sheriff thought for a moment. 'Good idea,' he said. 'I'll have to think about it though, we could end up lettin' 'em kill everyone on the stage.'

'Tell you what,' offered Brogan. 'You just point me in the direction the stage comes an' I'll ride out an' see what I can see. You bring the posse out an' I'll meet you somewhere's.'

'There's about five hours before it's due,' said Dempster. 'I'll give you three hours, then we meet at Jed Drake's place. You can't miss it, it's a sort of a mess of a ranch right underneath the cliffs on the trail.'

'Three hours! OK, I'm on my way!' He did not give Sheriff Dempster the chance to reply, leaping on his horse and riding quickly out of town.

'Forget it!' he said to himself. 'You got fifty dollars, that's enough to last quite a while.'

'I'm tempted,' he admitted, 'but I'm curious too. I wanna see what happens to Mitchell.'

'If his men get to the stage before you do, it ain't a case of what happens to Mitchell, it'll be a case of just how long you'll live. He'll try an' kill you for sure.'

'He can try!' he replied, confidently.

As usual, his conversation with himself resolved nothing other than what he had planned in the first place and he rode on, following the trail eastward. Half an hour later he came across what he assumed to be Jed Drake's ranch and Sheriff Dempster's assessment of it as a 'mess of buildings' was accurate enough; it did have a very run-down appearance. Brogan deliberately avoided the ranch, he had the feeling that he would not be too welcome. He would let the sheriff explain.

From the ranch onwards, the land started to rise and very soon he was among rolling hills, at first quite thickly covered in vegetation and trees, but slowly giving way to more open land. Brogan decided that it was time to take to the higher ground.

Brogan had years of experience in detecting people out in the open even from a great distance and he prided himself in that fact, but look and listen as hard as he might, he could not detect anything out of the ordinary for at least an hour. Suddenly he was alert, there was someone ahead of him who appeared to be coming towards him.

'Pete Cummins!' Brogan growled as the old man faced him. 'I might've guessed!'

'Hi there, Brogan,' Pete said, with a broad grin. 'You all by yourself?'

'For the moment,' replied Brogan.

'You still chasin' your money?'

'Could say that. I see you meant what you said 'bout not goin' back to Abbotsville.'

'Never more serious,' said Pete. 'Did you explain everythin' to Dempster?' Brogan nodded. 'I wish I'd heard it. I'll bet you was laughed out of town!'

'They was never more serious!' mocked Brogan. 'Right now I'm lookin' for whoever Mitchell hired, but I ain't havin' much luck so far, but I'll find 'em.'

'Might be able to help you there,' said Pete. 'I heard someone, about half an hour ago. They was headed north towards the trail. I heard one of 'em say somethin' about Big Bear Rock. That'd make sense, a perfect spot to ambush the stage.'

'Big Bear Rock?' asked Brogan. 'How far?'

'Ten miles north-west of here I'd say,' replied Pete.

'Thanks,' said Brogan. 'You don't have to leave town you know. Whatever happens, I reckon Mitchell is finished. You should be safe enough.'

'Naw!' Pete grinned. 'I've been thinkin' an' I had me a thought of this widder woman what used to fancy me up at Cedar Ridge. I reckon I might just go on up there an' look her up again.'

Brogan smiled. 'Why not, can't say as I blame you. I've thought about it more'n once. I reckon I could find me a few widders what'd like to see me again.'

'You oughta try it,' advised Pete. 'You ain't gettin' no younger an' it's about time you tried a few of life's comforts.'

'Only one thing puts me off,' admitted Brogan, 'baths! They all got this thing about gettin' me into the bath tub. Damn it, the last one succeeded as well, but I didn't use no soap!'

'Must've been one hell of a woman to do that!' Pete laughed.

'Yeh, she was,' admitted Brogan, 'but I was plastered in mud, there warn't no other way to get it off.'

'Well, that's what I'm gonna do,' said Pete. 'Bathin' or not, I'll take the chance.'

'Good luck!' called Brogan as he turned his horse.

He had no reason to doubt the accuracy of Pete's information and decided that he had better leave word at Jed Drake's ranch for Sheriff Dempster. He rode back quickly.

As he had expected, his arrival at the ranch was treated with deep mistrust. Jed Drake and a youth, whom Brogan assumed to be the son, kept their ancient rifles trained on him all the time.

'What you want, Mister?' demanded Jed Drake.

'You are Jed Drake ain't you?' asked Brogan.

'Who the hell we are ain't no concern of yours!' snapped the youth. 'He is the same one, Pa!'

'Sure looks like it,' agreed the older man. 'What is it you want, Mister? We saw you ride past earlier. Don't deny it, it was you, warn't it?'

'You got good eyesight,' said Brogan. 'Sure, it was me.'

'You musta seen I got a pretty wife an' daughter!' snarled Drake. 'Come back to take 'em have you?'

'Now hold it!' said Brogan, raising his hands. 'I'm

sure you do have a pretty wife an' daughter, but I
don't know nothin' 'bout them. I just came back to
leave a message for Sheriff Dempster.'

'There ain't no sheriff here!' snapped the youth.

'I know that,' said Brogan. 'But he'll be along
soon, I can assure you of that an' he'll be leadin' a
posse ... '

'An' they is after you!' exclaimed the youth.
'Maybe there's a reward out for you. We could
make a name for ourselves, Pa, an' some money.'

'Yeh!' Drake hissed through a mouthful of bad
teeth. 'Off your horse, Mister, we'll hold you for
the sheriff!'

'It ain't me that's wanted!' exclaimed Brogan.

'Pull the other one, Mister!' Drake hissed again.

With two rifles aimed steadily at him, even
though he could see that one of them was an
ancient muzzle loader, he was not really in a
position to argue, so he slowly started to
dismount. At that moment a woman, who could
hardly be described as 'pretty' came out of the
house. Both Drake and the youth turned and that
was enough for Brogan. A single shot sent the rifle
flying from Jed Drake's hand, but the youth was
quick to react and the single ball shot from the
ancient muzzle loader singed across Brogan's
shoulder.

'You just lost your only chance!' snarled Brogan,
levelling his Colt at them. Jed Drake clutched a
bleeding hand and screamed at the woman.

'Get back in the house! Get the other gun ... '

'When will some folk listen?' sighed Brogan.

'I've told you, I ain't after your women an' I ain't wanted by the sheriff! Now you just listen an' be sure to tell Dempster! You got that?' They both nodded dumbly. 'My name's McNally, he'll know. Tell him they is at Big Bear Rock, wherever that is.'

'Big Bear Rock?' croaked the youth. 'Who'll be out there?'

'That I don't know. Just tell him Big Bear Rock. How far is it from here?'

'About an hour's ride,' hissed Jed Drake.

'Then I gotta be goin'!' said Brogan. 'You just be sure to tell Dempster, that's all, he'll know what it's all about!' He remounted his horse and swung her round just as the youth went to grab hold of the rifle shot from his father's hands. Brogan's bullet was quicker then the youth and the rifle butt shattered and the rifle span harmlessly away. 'That could've been your head!' warned Brogan. 'It will be next time!' He rode off, leaving a bewildered youth and an equally bewildered Jed Drake nursing a deep scratch on his hand.

Brogan had little difficulty in recognizing Big Bear Rock. From the three or four miles he must have been from it, it did indeed look like an enormous bear. Having established where it was, he left the trail for the higher ground again.

He reasoned that Sheriff Dempster would have received the message and be on his way by now, but he had no real idea what time it was; time of the day meant very little. He had had a watch once, but it had eventually refused to work and he

had always been quite convinced it told the wrong
time. It was fairly easy going and he was able to
look down on the trail and cast an eagle eye over
every likely ambush point. It was not until he was
almost alongside Big Bear Rock that he saw them.

He whistled softly to himself, although he was
not too surprised. Apart from Steve Bates, the
man from the mine, there were three others all of
whom he recognized as the three who had robbed
Pete Cummins. His whistle had not been so much
due to the fact of recognizing them, but the fact
that they were, at that moment, changing their
clothes for those of the half-breeds; at least, three
of them were. The fourth, Steve Bates, was in the
scanty garb worn by Red Wolf.

It would have been very easy for him to kill all
four of them from where he was – they obviously
had no idea that they were being watched – but
he decided against it. He was well placed to act if
anything went wrong.

From his vantage point, he could see quite a
distance along the shallow valley in either
direction and so far there was no indication of
either the stage or the sheriff's posse, but then he
would have been quite disappointed if the sheriff
had shown up.

He suddenly gripped his rifle and held his
breath as one of the men below started to climb up
towards him, but the man stopped when he was
about half way and began to scan the eastern end
of the valley, obviously looking for the stagecoach.
He waited for about twenty minutes before

suddenly calling to the others. Brogan had seen
the dust raised by the approaching stage before
the man below.

'About fifteen minutes!' Brogan muttered to
himself, looking the opposite direction for Sheriff
Dempster.

The first sign of the approaching sheriff and his
posse came as the stage was about two hundred
yards from the waiting men, which meant that
they would arrive on the scene about ten minutes
after they had struck. Brogan fought back the
instinct to strike first.

Two of the men rode out either side of the stage,
which was not travelling too fast and the other
two straddled the trail, blocking its path. Brogan
could see that the driver thought about whipping
the horses into a gallop but then thought better of
it when he saw the two ahead of him. The stage
ground to a halt without a shot being fired.

Brogan was too far away to hear exactly what
was being said, but the coach driver nodded to the
rear and two of them began to rummage through
the luggage strapped to the back, eventually
finding what they were looking for – two small
metal boxes. For good measure the three
passengers were ordered to give up their
valuables and a couple of trunks were forced open
and their contents scattered about. A few items
were pocketed, despite protests from the passengers, three men.

Suddenly Steve Bates, dressed as an Indian,

was shouting and pointing and the two not already on horseback raced to their animals and mounted, turning and heading directly towards Brogan, two of them clutching one box each. Brogan decided that it was time to act.

His first two shots sent two men spinning from their horses, the two carrying the boxes. The other two dragged their horses to a halt, Steve Bates pulling too hard and pulling his horse over. The other managed to recover and turn back to head along the valley away from the rapidly approaching posse. His dash for freedom was short-lived as three of the posse broke away and very quickly overhauled him.

Brogan had slithered down the hillside and now had the three other men covered. Sheriff Dempster joined him and looked down scornfully at the three.

'Looks like you bungled it again!' he sneered.

The two injured men had shoulder wounds and struggled to their feet where they glared in hatred at Brogan. Steve Bates seemed totally confused.

'You again!' snarled one of the men.

'Yeh, me again!' Brogan grinned. 'Only thing is, this time I don't reckon your friend Mitchell is gonna be able to let you go.'

'Friend! He ain't no friend of ours. This is all his fault!'

'We know that,' said Dempster, 'but you can tell us all about it back in town. I'll get the doc to see to your shoulders.'

'Tell me somethin',' one of them snarled at Brogan. 'You got a crystal ball or somethin'?'

'Somethin' like that!' Brogan laughed.

TEN

The coach passengers were allowed to recover their possessions and the four would-be robbers were set astride their horses with their hands tied behind them. The stage continued its journey, this time flanked by the posse. Brogan took up a position some distance behind and was eventually joined by Sheriff Dempster.

'You sure gave Jed Drake somethin' to think about,' said Dempster. 'When we left him he was still convinced we were chasin' you an' he still reckoned you were after his women.'

'Don't know about the daughter,' said Brogan, with a wry smile, 'I didn't see her, but I saw his wife. He said she was pretty, but she sure warn't my idea of pretty. She looked like she weighed about two hundred pounds.'

'About right I'd say,' replied Dempster. 'Rose, his daughter, is about the same size as her. Old Jed is always quite convinced that every man in the territory is chasin' after 'em. Rose could've gotten herself a husband a few times, but he always ended up scarin' 'em off. It's a good job you didn't wait for us, there'd've been a good chance they might've got away.'

'I didn't know how long it'd take you to get here, so I figured someone'd better be around. 'Sides, it was a whole lot healthier than stayin' there. I don't reckon I could ever have convinced Drake.'

Dempster laughed. 'I'll lay odds that he still don't believe we warn't after you. Once he's got somethin' set in his mind there ain't no shiftin' it.'

As they passed Jed Drake's ranch, the sheriff's opinion was confirmed as Jed and his son stood at the side of the trail.

'See you caught him, Sheriff!' called Drake. 'Good thing too. No woman is safe with folk like him around. I want him charged with assault too ...' He raised a bandaged hand. 'Shattered my hand he did, I'll never be able to use it again!'

'It ain't your drinkin' hand!' Dempster laughed. They rode on and he spoke to Brogan. 'He'll use that injury to the best advantage. He won't be able to do nothin' on the ranch an' he'll try an' use it to bum drinks in the saloon. He may get a few drinks out of it, but not for long. Folks are used to him by now.'

They reached Abbotsville just as the sun was dipping below the western horizon and their arrival brought the whole town to life. There was a great deal of speculation as to what Mitchell would do about the men. Everyone knew that they either did or had worked for him. However, the extent of Mitchell's involvement was known only to Brogan, the sheriff and Evans and that was the way Dempster wanted to keep it.

The prisoners were quickly ushered away and locked up and the doc called to attend their injuries. The doc asked no questions and the men did not say anything while he was there. It was after the doc had fixed their shoulders and had left that Mr Evans and the sheriff got together. Evans even tolerated Brogan's presence.

'If you've got my money, I'll be on my way!' said Brogan.

'I do not carry that kind of money on me!' said Evans, sniffing at Brogan. 'It is you! I wasn't wrong the first time!'

'It was me!' Brogan grinned. 'So when do I get my money?'

'In the morning!' replied Evans. 'Now, Sheriff. Have you questioned these men yet?'

'I haven't really had chance,' said Dempster, 'we'll do it now.'

The three of them went through into the cells where they were met by a hostile silence.

'What were you told to look for when you robbed the stage?' asked Evans. 'You might as well admit the truth, we know you were under orders from Mitchell.'

'If you know that much, you must know what we were lookin' for!' snapped Steve Bates.

'It is quite plain that the passengers in the stage were supposed to think they had been attacked by Red Wolf and his gang,' continued Evans. 'We have found their bodies.'

'Then I suppose you'll be includin' murder

charges as well as holdin' up the stage!' snarled one of the others.

'It is quite possible,' agreed Evans.

'On the other hand you've probably done us all a favour in gettin' rid of 'em,' said Dempster. 'I reckon if you confess to Mitchell bein' the instigator, we could quite easily forget about the bodies under that tree. They're well off the trail an' it could be a long time afore anyone finds what's left of 'em. As far as everyone else is concerned they just decided to quit the territory. It's your choice, we've got enough evidence either way to have you put inside the State Pen for a long time.'

The men all looked at each other and slowly nodded. 'OK, Sheriff we'll tell you everythin'. You promise mind, you'll see to it that we get a fair hearin' an' not too long in prison.'

'I'll do what I can,' assured Dempster. 'I can't promise anythin', how long you get is up to the judge, not me.'

'No, but you've got influence with him!' said Bates.

'Some,' admitted Dempster. 'I reckon he'll listen to what I've got to say.'

'OK, it's a deal,' agreed Bates.

Their story, although varying in very minor detail, was almost exactly as Brogan had surmised. Mitchell had hit upon the idea of using the payroll money after the attempt to rob Pete Cummins and he had promised them five hundred each to carry out the robbery on the stage. The

idea of killing Red Wolf and his gang was nothing
to do with Mitchell, that had happened due to a
dispute between them. When they had finished
their story, one of them asked Dempster just how
Brogan figured in it all.

'That's where Mitchell made his biggest
mistake,' said Dempster. 'McNally here wasn't
nothin' to do with it. It was pure chance he came
along after you'd robbed Cummins. If Mitchell
had left it alone at that, maybe everythin'
would've been all right. Don't know why he did it,
but he hired McNally to take the payroll to the
mine.'

"Ceptin' it warn't the payroll!' added Brogan.

'Which is why I can't understand him hirin'
you,' said Dempster.

'I think I can explain,' said Evans. 'I am afraid I
had insisted that someone more reliable than Pete
Cummins had to be used. Someone who knew how
to handle himself and a gun. I am afraid that Mr
McNally was the only choice.'

'Well that explains that!' said Dempster. 'OK,
you've kept your part of the bargain, I'll see what I
can do with the judge.'

Back in the office, Brogan was smiling to
himself. 'I guess I had you figured wrong, Sheriff,'
he said. 'I had you so deep in Mitchell's pocket you
couldn't find your way out.'

'So did he,' said Dempster. 'I went along with
him because it was the best way. I never was
really behind him. Don't get me wrong, he wasn't
all bad, he's spent a lot of money on this town, but

he was beginnin' to get power-mad. He needed bringin' down a bit, but it's a pity in a way that it had to be like this.'

'I agree with you Sheriff,' said Evans. 'But he had brought it on himself. Had he confined his activities to ranching he would not have been in the mess he is. He was advised, even warned, not to become involved in the mine, but he insisted. His other interests are all highly successful. It is the mine which has been such a drain on his finances. The fifty thousand you know about is only a small part of his debt but, unfortunately for him, it is the part which is secured against his ranch. He had fallen so far behind with his payments that my superiors ordered foreclosure.'

'All too complicated for me!' Brogan laughed. 'That's why I'm a hobo, you ain't got no worries like that. All you need is enough to get by.'

By the look Evans gave to Brogan, it was quite plain that he did not agree with him.

'Steve should've been back by now,' said Jim Harker. 'Somethin' must've gone wrong.'

'What could possibly go wrong?' asked Mitchell. 'Holding up a stage is child's play.'

'Maybe someone started shootin' back,' suggested Harker. 'If everythin' had gone all right, he should have been back here by now.'

'It was you who said he could be trusted,' said Mitchell. 'I took your word for it. I'll tell you what I think. I think he found more on that stage than he expected. I have heard that quite sizeable amounts of money get transported from time to time. I'll wager that it was one of those times and they've run out with it.'

'Then I reckon you could have a problem,' said Harker.

'Only if they did nothing about the deeds,' said Mitchell. 'If they've destroyed those, that's all I'm concerned about. I don't care how much money the stage was carrying.'

'So how are you goin' to find out?' asked Harker.

'I'm not, you are!' retorted Mitchell.

'Me!'

'Yes, you!' repeated Mitchell. 'You are going into Abbotsville ahead of me to find out if anything went wrong.'

'And if it did?'

'Then you ride back and tell me.'

'What'll you do if it did?'

'That depends on what it was,' said Mitchell. 'We'll both ride back but you go on when we're close to town. Don't worry, there's absolutely nothing to connect you with anything. You can always say you were looking for me.'

'OK,' agreed Harker. 'I guess you're right, I've done nothin' wrong.'

It was another day before Harker and Mitchell overlooked Abbotsville, two days after the attempt on the stage. Brogan had been paid his money, as promised, but instead of leaving town, he had decided to hang about and see what happened.

'Jim Harker is ridin' in!' announced Dempster, who had been on the lookout for someone. 'Since you're still here, McNally, play it cool, pretend you are still waitin' for Mitchell to show up and pay you. It'd be best if you were to meet him outside of town, down by the corrals. You can spin him some yarn, whatever you think fit, but if he comes into town I'll have to arrest him. I want him to get back to Mitchell, it's Mitchell I want, not Harker.'

'Glad to be of service,' said Brogan. He walked quickly down to the corrals and waited about ten minutes for Jim Harker to arrive.

'You still here?' asked Harker, rather surprised to see Brogan.

'Mitchell still owes me some money,' said Brogan. 'He knows I'm waitin' for it.'

'I was hopin' to see Mr Mitchell myself,' said Harker. 'I thought he would be in town.'

'Ain't seen hair nor hide of him,' said Brogan. 'He's missed all the fun.'

'Fun! What fun?' demanded Harker.

'Seems that bunch of renegade Indians held up the stage a couple of days back,' said Brogan. 'Didn't kill nobody, but they took a whole heap of money an' things, includin' some mighty important documents, accordin' to Mr Evans from the bank.'

'Money! How much money?' asked Harker.

'Evans won't say exactly,' said Brogan, 'but they reckon it was somethin' like a hundred thousand.'

Harker whistled and smiled. 'They took some documents as well? Have they been found yet?'

'Oh, sure!' Brogan grinned. Harker looked quite alarmed. 'They used 'em to light a fire. All that's left is a pile of ash!'

'It ain't the first time the stage has been robbed,' said Harker. 'I don't expect it's gonna be the last. You say Mitchell ain't in town?' Brogan shook his head. 'Then there ain't much point in me goin' in there. He should've been here though, he left before I did. Maybe somethin's happened to him along the trail an' I missed him. I'll ride back an' take a look.'

'Want some help?' suggested Brogan.

'Er ... er ... no thanks,' faltered Harker. 'You'd best stay here in case he shows up. You can tell him I want to see him, the Chinese are givin' me some trouble an' I need him to sort it out.'

'I'll do that,' agreed Brogan. 'An' if you see him first, you can tell him I'm gettin' mighty impatient about my money.'

'You'll get your money!' assured Harker, turning his horse and riding back the way he had come.

'Nice work,' said Dempster when Brogan returned. 'What you tell him?'

'I told him the stage had been robbed an' that about a hundred thousand had been stolen an' some valuable documents destroyed. He seemed to buy it. He said Mitchell had left before him and he was looking for him.'

'And do you believe that?'

'Not a word!' Brogan grinned. 'He was sent ahead by Mitchell to check. I reckon you'll be seein' Mitchell before too long.'

'A hundred thousand!' exclaimed Mitchell. 'Jeez! No wonder they ran out on us. So Brogan reckons they've destroyed the documents. I only hope he's right.'

'You can count on it,' assured Harker. 'Steve may have run out with the cash, an' who the hell wouldn't with that amount, but he would've destroyed them deeds. That's what you told him to do if he had to, wasn't it? I've known him a long time, he'll keep to his end of the bargain knowin' that you won't put the finger on him. I don't know how he did it, but McNally reckons it was them renegades who took the stage. I'll guarantee it was Steve.'

'I don't much care who it was,' said Mitchell, 'just so long as those deeds can never get back to Evans or the bank. I told you the stage sometimes carried a lot of money. A hundred thousand! I could've used that myself.'

'Couldn't we all!' agreed Harker.

'I see you found him,' greeted Brogan as Mitchell and Harker rode into town. 'You got my money?'

'You'll get it!' snarled Mitchell.

'Hi there, Mr Mitchell!' called out a passer-by. 'I guess you heard about the stage bein' held up!'

'I heard,' replied Mitchell. The confirmation that the stage had been held up seemed to please him and he rode on full of confidence. He was met outside the bank by Mr Evans.

'Good afternoon, Seth,' greeted Evans. 'I trust you are in a position to pay your debt?'

'I'll pay just as soon as you can hand over those deeds,' replied Mitchell. 'I hear the stage was robbed an' they got away with about a hundred thousand and some documents.'

'Ah, you have heard!' Mr Evans was playing his part very well and Brogan had to smile. 'Yes, there was a little difficulty. It was not a hundred thousand, only ninety four thousand.'

'I don't suppose those renegades are going to worry too much about six thousand!' Mitchell laughed.

'Renegades! Ah yes,' sighed Evans. 'I do believe the sheriff would like a word with you about that.'

'Yeh, I agree,' said Mitchell. 'This time they've gone too far. I expect he wants to form a posse to go after them. I'm all for it. The sooner we are rid of them the better.'

'It's not as simple as that,' said Evans, 'the Indian Affairs Department have to be involved. I'm not certain why the sheriff wants to speak to you, but I know it's important.'

'I'll go see him right away!' Mitchell grinned. 'I don't suppose he wants to see you, Jim. Why not treat yourself to a drink in the saloon? In fact you can have this one on me!' He tossed Harker a silver dollar. Harker took the hint and the dollar and headed for the saloon. Mitchell hitched his horse outside the sheriff's office and went inside, closely followed by Brogan.

'You want to see me?' Mitchell beamed, full of

confidence.

'Afternoon, Mr Mitchell,' greeted Dempster. 'Everythin' all right up at the mine? I hear you were havin' trouble with the Chinese.'

'Nothin' that can't be sorted out,' said Mitchell. 'I hear the stage was robbed, a hundred thousand or thereabouts.'

'Yeh, someone dressed like Indians,' said Dempster.

'Dressed like Indians?'

'That's right. We know they warn't Indians though,' said Dempster. 'Brogan here found the bodies of Red Wolf an' his band, all very dead.'

'Then who was it?' asked Mitchell, looking at Brogan with some distaste.

'I thought maybe you'd know,' said Dempster.

'Why the hell should I know anythin' like that? I've been up at the mine, as McNally here can testify.'

'Never said you wasn't,' said Dempster, walking to the door through to the cells. 'I wanna show you somethin'.'

'I'm intrigued!' said Mitchell, rather nervously. He followed the sheriff through the door and almost immediately he tried to rush back, at the same time drawing his gun. His progress was stopped at the door when Brogan's Colt was rammed up his nose.

'In a hurry?' asked Brogan.

'I ... I ... I just remembered some very important business!' faltered Mitchell.

'I'd say you got more important business right

here,' said Brogan. 'F'rinstance, why are they dressed up like they are?'

'How should I know?' croaked Mitchell.

'They say you paid them to rob the stage!' said Dempster.

'Then they're lying!' blustered Mitchell. 'Scum like that'll say anything to save their own skins. I fired three of them, remember!'

'An' Steve Bates?' prompted Dempster.

'Him too!' Mitchell croaked. 'We had a row up at the mine and he rode out.'

'You told me he'd gone to the railroad,' said Brogan.

'That was purely for your benefit!' said Mitchell. 'I wasn't going to tell the likes of you my business.'

'Was you gonna tell anyone about there only bein' paper in that satchel?' asked Brogan.

'What are you talking about?' bluffed Mitchell. 'You told us Red Wolf took it off you!'

'So he did,' agreed Brogan, 'but you an' me both know all he got was paper.'

'You surely don't believe this do you, Sheriff? Call Jim Harker, he was there. Ask Steve Bates too. I'm beginning to wonder if Cummins and McNally didn't divide it between themselves.'

For the first time, there was a look of doubt in Dempster's face as he looked at Brogan.

'Ain't no cause to look at me like that, Sheriff,' said Brogan. 'If that'd been the case, I'd've been long gone from here. I reckon you'll find the money either in his office or his house.'

'I've had enough of this nonsense!' Mitchell

growled. 'You'll have to excuse me, I have important work to do!'

'Sorry,' said Dempster. 'You're goin' nowhere, not yet awhile. Them four in there all made statements sayin' you put 'em up to it. That's enough for me. What happens now is up to the lawyers.'

'You mean you're holding me in there, with them?'

'Not with them!' said the sheriff. 'There is another cell out the back, you know that.'

The office door opened and Jim Harker burst in, looking rather wild eyed. He looked with alarm at the gun in Brogan's hand and at the sheriff. 'I just heard about Steve an' the others!' he exclaimed. 'I just want you to know I had nothin' at all to do with it! It was all his idea!' He nodded at Mitchell.

'Bastard!' screamed Mitchell, who still had his gun. He levelled it at Harker but it was knocked from his hand by Brogan.

Mr Evans pushed his way past Jim Harker and thrust a document in front of Mitchell. 'Your deeds, Mr Mitchell. You can have them on payment of fifty thousand dollars!'

Mitchell looked with pure hatred at Brogan. Suddenly he spat in his face. 'Bastard! This is all your fault! If it hadn't been for you, Evans, insisting that someone else take the money with Cummins I would never have hired him. I don't know where you've come from or where you're goin' to, McNally, but you should never have come through this town! It's all your fault!'

Brogan laughed. 'All I ever do is mind my own business an' I still get the blame for everythin'! That's OK, I don't mind, someone's gotta be blamed I suppose!'